THE DEVIL YOU KNOW

✦✦✦✦✦✦✦✦✦✦✦✦✦✦✦✦✦✦✦✦

THE DEVIL YOU KNOW

✦✦✦✦✦✦✦✦✦✦✦✦✦✦✦✦✦✦

POPPY Z. BRITE

GAUNTLET PUBLICATIONS
■ 2005 ■

Gauntlet Tradepaperback Edition
ISBN 1-887368-77-9
The Devil You Know © 2005 by Poppy Z. Brite
Cover Art © 2005 by Alan M. Clark
Cover Layout by Gail Cross
Interior Page Design by Dara Hoffman

Subterranean Press Signed/Limited Edition
The Devil You Know © 2003 by Poppy Z. Brite

"Dispatches from Tanganyika: A Foreword" © 2003, 2005 by Poppy Z. Brite, appears here for the first time.

"The Devil You Know" (© 2000 by Poppy Z. Brite) was originally published in *Imagination Fully Dilated 2*.

"O Death, Where Is Thy Spatula?" (© 2001 by Poppy Z. Brite) was originally published in *The Spook*.

"Lantern Marsh" (© 2000 by Poppy Z. Brite) was originally published in *October Dreams*.

"Nothing of Him That Doth Fade" (© 2000 by Poppy Z. Brite) was originally published in *Aqua Erotica*.

"The Ocean" (© 2002 by Poppy Z. Brite) was originally published in *Darker Side*.

"Marisol" (© 2001 by Poppy Z. Brite) was originally published on www.gothic.net.

"Poivre" (© 2002 by Poppy Z. Brite) was originally published as part of a longer piece in *The Spook*.

"Pansu" (© 2001 by Poppy Z. Brite) was originally published as a limited-edition chapbook by Camelot Books.

"Burn, Baby, Burn" (© 1999 by Mike Mignola) was originally published in *Hellboy: Odd Jobs*.

"System Freeze" (© 1999 by Warner Bros.) was originally published on www.whatisthematrix.com.
"Bayou de la Mère" (© 2002 by Poppy Z. Brite) was originally published in *Queer Fear 2*.

"The Heart of New Orleans" (© 2002 by Poppy Z. Brite) was originally published in *City Slab*.

"A Season in Heck" © 2003 by Poppy Z. Brite appears here for the first time.

All rights reserved.

This book, or parts thereof, may not be reproduced in any form without permission in writing from the publisher.

This book is a work of fiction. Names, characters, places and incidents are either the products of the author's imagination or are used fictitiously. Any resemblance to actual events or locations or persons, living or dead, is entirely coincidental.

Manufactured in the United States of America
EDGE BOOKS
An Imprint of Gauntlet Press
Gauntlet Publications
5307 Arroyo Street
Colorado Springs, CO 80922
United States of America
Phone: (719) 591-5566
email: info@gauntletpress.com
Website: www.gauntletpress.com

Author's website: www.poppyzbrite.com

For Harlan Ellison,
who's helped me longer than he's known me,

and Kirin Anderson,
who helps me more than she knows

Acknowledgments

Special thanks to Duncan Bock, Connie Brite, Jennifer Caudle, Richard Chizmar, Alan M. Clark, Geoff Cooper, Richard Curtis, Christopher DeBarr, Tony and Kim Duarte, Betsy Engstrom, Christa Faust, Shayne Fenton, David Ferguson, Joel Fletcher, Neil Gaiman, Christopher Golden, John Harris, Barry Hoffman, Caitlín R. Kiernan, Spencer Lamm, Eman Loubier, Louis Maistros, Gerard Maras, Thom Maras, Darren Mckeeman, Mike Mignola, Frank Minyard, Mary Ann Mohanraj, Bob Morrish, John Pelan, Michael Rowe, Bill Schafer, David J. Schow, Jamie Shannon, Ira Silverberg, Tenacious D, Tulane University, Kevin Unsell, Pete and Janis Vazquez, the Wachowski Brothers, and Drew Zeigler.

TABLE OF CONTENTS
✦✦✦✦✦✦✦✦✦✦✦✦✦✦✦✦✦✦✦

DISPATCHES FROM TANGANYIKA: A FOREWORD	11
THE DEVIL YOU KNOW	19
O DEATH, WHERE IS THY SPATULA?	27
LANTERN MARSH	43
NOTHING OF HIM THAT DOTH FADE	55
THE OCEAN	67
MARISOL	77
POIVRE	87
PANSU	91
BURN, BABY, BURN	101
SYSTEM FREEZE	111
BAYOU DE LA MÈRE	117
THE HEART OF NEW ORLEANS	131
A SEASON IN HECK	143

DISPATCHES FROM TANGANYIKA:
A FOREWORD

This is my third short story collection, and to me it seems the most schizophrenic. I don't mean that it is uneven: I hope it's not. What I mean is that although most of these stories were written over the course of just four years, I think of them as being divided into two distinct camps, with one story that straddles the two camps and perhaps attempts to negotiate peace between them (I'm not sure whether it succeeds—I suppose that's for you to decide).

Between 1997 and 2000, I experienced something that didn't feel so much like writer's block as writer's *fatigue*. I was writing, but it came very slowly and never really gave me the high I get when the work's going well. I worked for two years on something that had been conceived as a novel, but only ended up being about 90 pages long. I wrote a number of short stories that I thought were good, but only because I'd learned to write competently in the absence of real passion. I wrote a number of short stories that I thought were terrible (none of these appear here). I started another novel, but completed only two chapters over the course of two months, with every word feeling like an attempt to squeeze blood out of a cut that's trying to heal.

Finally in the fall of 2000 I was so sick of myself and my moribund novel that I decided to write something else, something that would just be fun. This "fun book" turned out to be *Liquor*, which was published in 2004 by Three Rivers Press, and it ended up changing everything I thought I knew about writing. Probably those changes were happening anyway, over those years that I felt so tired, and *Liquor* was just the conscious culmination of them. But in the course of writing it, I realized I was tired of always dealing with damaged, angst-ridden characters; that I was tired of writing horror, a field that had once felt boundless to me; and most of all that I was deeply dissatisfied with the way I'd been writing about New Orleans.

I was born here in 1967, lived here until I was six, and visited every few years until I moved back for good in 1993. After returning, it took me a few more years to realize I'd never understood the city very well despite having written three novels about it. Though there are still things I like very much about each of those novels, I began to feel that they revealed little about the real fabric of the city: rather, they fed into the web of spooky-gorgeous-decadent-dangerous clichés that mars so much New Orleans fiction. That side of the city does exist, but it's a small side, and to me it has become a relatively dull one. I'm more interested now in the people who lead ordinary New Orleans lives, with no vampires or serial killers to spice things up. We don't need those things – an ordinary life in New Orleans is so different from one lived anywhere else that the accoutrements of fantasy fiction begin to seem superfluous after a while. Probably the best piece of fiction ever written about New Orleans, and certainly the truest, is John Kennedy Toole's *A Confederacy of Dunces*. This novel reads like an absurdist fantasy to people who live elsewhere, but New Orleanians recognize every one of its characters—we see them, and hear them, constantly.

Liquor was the first time I tried to write at novel length about a New Orleans I'd really seen and heard, not one I'd fantasized about. Whether I did a good job is up to the reader, but

I enjoyed the attempt so much that I wrote another novel (*The Value of X*) about the early years of the characters and their families, then a novella about them, then a number of short stories, and a third novel, *Prime*. There will be at least two more novels; I intend to keep writing about these characters for a long time. It may seem strange to latch onto characters so obsessively, but I've begun to hope that I can speak truly about New Orleans by chronicling the lives of some ordinary people who've been shaped by the place—not tourists, not fugitives, not supernatural entities, just a couple of hard-working cooks who want to make good food. I don't know if readers will like this reality as well as they liked my silly, gorgeous, decadent fantasy of New Orleans. When John Kennedy Toole submitted *A Confederacy of Dunces* to a New York publisher, he got the following response: "[W]hen someone like yourself is living off from the center of cultural-business activities, with only a thin lifeline to that center, through vague and solitary contacts, everything gets disproportionate, difficult to analyze, to give the proper weight to. It is like those odd people who turn up in New Zealand or Tanganyika or Finland, writing or painting masterpieces—they have their own power, but they read or look as if the artist has had to discover the form for himself. They don't have the assurance of worldliness and mutual interest and energy with others."*

Now this can be interpreted in a number of ways, none of them good as far as I can see. To me it sounds like a kiss-off on the basis of truth, a dismissal of a New Orleans novel that's not about Mardi Gras or voodoo or Hurricanes or dinners at Antoine's; hell, it's not even particularly sultry. I may be wrong. Gottlieb himself seemed to realize he wasn't being terribly clear: "I don't know what I've just said here, and I don't know that I want to turn back to see (a Lot's wife complex)."** But it has always struck me as rather easy to make readers believe fiction that wallows in the clichés of New

---

* Letter to John Kennedy Toole from Robert Gottlieb, senior editor at Simon & Schuster, March 23, 1965

** ibid.

Orleans, and not so easy to make them believe fiction that approaches the truth of the place. The truth, after all, is far stranger than the clichés.

So the stories in this book are roughly divided, in my mind, into pre-*Liquor* and post-*Liquor* stories. I haven't arranged them that way, since attention must be paid to things like flow and juxtaposition when determining a collection's order, but the following notes will tell you a little about how some of the stories came about and where they fall in my personal chronology. A few of them might possibly tell you more about the stories than you want to know—if you're one of those people who prefers to read fiction "cold," skip this section until later or just ignore it altogether.

"The Devil You Know" was written in 1999 for *Imagination Fully Dilated*, an anthology of fiction inspired by the surreal artwork of Alan M. Clark. I chose to write about a painting of a giant, funny-looking cat sprawled on the black and white tile floor of a large room. The floor reminded me of my bathroom, which gave me the idea that the cat was in New Orleans, and I'd just read Mikhail Bulgakov's *The Master and Margarita*, which gave me the idea that the cat belonged to the Devil. Somehow this turned into a story about the racism of the old-line Carnival krewes. Sharp-eyed readers will spot a character from my novel *Exquisite Corpse*, albeit in his early years.

"O Death, Where Is Thy Spatula?" is the second story in my series about my alternate life as Dr. Brite, the coroner of New Orleans. It is also a spell that didn't work. In the summer of 2001 I learned that a chef friend of mine was dying of cancer. I took a break from *Liquor* to write a story about trying to bring a chef back from the dead. My friend died in November, and though I like the story, I will never be able to feel that it was a complete success.

"Lantern Marsh" is a reworking of a story I wrote long ago, before I'd even made my first sale—1983 or '84, perhaps. It received an honorable mention in *Twilight Zone*'s annual short story contest, and I was always fond of it. In 1999 I was typing up some old "trunk" stories for a section of my website that featured previously unpublished juvenilia. This section was meant as a curiosity, not as good fiction, and

I decided I liked "Lantern Marsh" too much to consign it to the rejection-slip pile. Instead, I rewrote it and sold it to *October Dreams*, a wonderful big anthology of Halloween stories edited by Richard Chizmar and Robert Morrish.

"Nothing Of Him That Doth Fade" was written in late 1999 when I was about as depressed as I've ever been. I still don't much like to talk about it.

"The Ocean" grew out of a conversation I had with Neil Gaiman about fame, mythology, cannibalism, and Led Zeppelin. Early reader reactions to the story caused me to post a mini-diatribe on my website: "Please get yourself a rudimentary classical education, or at least find out about Orpheus and the Maenads, before reading this story. If one more person thinks it's about vampires, I may shoot myself in despair at the ignorance of young American horror readers." It is my last rock'n'roll story, at least for the foreseeable future—I'm sick to death of musicians.

"Marisol" is the third Dr. Brite story. It's also a real restaurant, and you can visit it at 437 Esplanade Avenue, New Orleans, or at www.marisolrestaurant.com.

"Poivre" is my attempt to emulate the work of my favorite food writer, M.F.K. Fisher. She wrote all sorts of things, but some of my favorite pieces are very short meditations on restaurants that had played an important part in her life—usually places she could no longer visit for one reason or another. It's a true story, but I attempted to turn myself into the sort of spoiled, insufferable character I sometimes feel like when I've been overindulging in restaurant meals.

I think the seed of "Pansu" must have been a scene in Darren Mckeeman's wildly imaginative, funny, as-yet-published novel *City of Apocrypha*. Aside from a *South Park*-related sexual fantasy that shall go undiscussed here, I can't imagine what else would have made me want to write about Satanic possession in an Asian restaurant in California. At the time of writing—the summer of 2000—the story seemed like a way of paying tribute to a beloved Korean restaurant that had closed. I read it recently and thought, "This was a tribute?" Those were strange times, just before I gave up writing the depressing novel and started the fun one. I'd recently visited Los Angeles. I'd almost entirely quit writing about New Orleans, thinking I had nothing left to say about it—other stories I wrote around this time were set in Australia, Tibet, and Nashville (!). I had two characters I liked pretty well, a pair of comedy writers. I wrote "Pansu." It's far from the best story I've ever written, but I include it here because I think of it as a sort of divider between the two camps of stories in this book. After a lot of difficult nonfiction pieces and fiction that was grim in every sense of the word, "Pansu" showed me that I could still thoroughly enjoy writing.

The next two stories are what Caitlín R. Kiernan calls "from weird and distant shores"—less poetically, they're my ideas plunked down in someone else's fictional world. Many writers sneer at this practice, but I enjoy it...occasionally. "Burn, Baby, Burn" was written in 1998 for an anthology of stories about Mike Mignola's comic *Hellboy*. When editor Chris Golden invited me to write one, I never in a million years thought I'd want to do it, but I let him send me the comics because I love free comics. But I really liked the pyrokinetic character Liz Sherman, and I include "Burn, Baby, Burn" here because I think it's one of the better things I've written about a female character—probably because I didn't have to invent her.

"System Freeze" was written—also in 1998—for whatisthematrix.com, the website of the popular film *The Matrix*. It is set in that film's world, but the characters are mine. Sometimes I think this story makes no sense at all; sometimes I think it turned out a lot better than I had any right to expect. I'm vacillating even as I type.

The final three stories are set firmly back in my own world—the current one of New Orleans restaurants and families. "Bayou de la Mère" is the most recent story in the collection. Conceived on a trip through the strange, fertile, religious territory of south Louisiana, it has to do with something that began to haunt me as I wrote about a large Catholic family and their son who'd left the Church many years ago: how does childhood religion scar you, and is there any strength to be gained from it even after you've lost your faith?

There's a family connection between "The Heart of New Orleans" and the *Value of X*/Liquor characters, but it doesn't really matter: primarily this is a Dr. Brite story that grew out of my research on *A Confederacy of Dunces*, its author, and his mother, Thelma Ducoing Toole, who got the novel published after her son's death. Reams of their papers and other artifacts are stored in the Manuscripts Collection at Tulane University, and I was going through them (for personal reasons as much as anything else) when I found Ken Toole's baby book, carefully created and preserved by his mother between 1937 and 1945 or so. Among the snapshots and crayon drawings were a lock of his hair and his first baby tooth. Toole was 31 when he died, but as my friend Louis pointed out after reading this story, "You see five-year-old teeth from a dead man, you think dead five-year-old."

The closer, "A Season in Heck," was intended as a short story but grew into a huge honking novella. Set mostly at Liquor (the restaurant) after they've been open for about a year, it centers not on my two main characters but on Paul, a desultory young cook with a lot of confusion in his life. Somewhat retrospectively autobiographical, somewhat influenced by Bruce Jay Friedman's novel *Stern*, Paul is maybe a bit of a throwback to my earlier characters—not as self-destructive and not nearly as fashionable, but more angst-ridden than anyone else I've written about in some time, almost a send-up of a Sensitive Young Fellow. I quite like him, though, despite the fact that my husband pronounced him a "weenie." (My husband has spent 25 years in restaurant kitchens, and I think he was just disgusted by the fact that Paul couldn't take the heat.)

So let's say that one day in October 2000 I woke up and realized I'd been living in Tanganyika. Most of these stories are dispatches from that strange land, attempts to set up a lamp and a desk and get comfortable, since I like it too much to leave. I hope they tell you something true about the place. It's been lied about enough; the truth is more interesting, even if we only have a thin lifeline to the center of the world. Perhaps that's all we need.

—Poppy Z. Brite
New Orleans, LA
June 2005

THE DEVIL YOU KNOW

Mr. Bulgakov knew of them as early as 1928, but their machinations combined with those of his native Russia made it impossible for him to publish his novel about them during his lifetime. When it was finally released decades later, everyone assumed it was fiction. So when the Devil and his great black cat came to New Orleans in 1985, no one at all was expecting them.

They took a large, fine house in the Garden District. There was an overgrown yard fenced in wrought iron and fringed with giant oaks where the cat could romp undetected. There was a porch where the Devil could sit sipping martinis spiked with Tabasco and observing the human show on St. Charles Avenue. The Devil acquainted himself with New Orleans society. Soon he was invited to join a prestigious Mardi Gras organization, the Krewe of Onan, which precipitated an argument at home.

"I insist upon riding in the parade with you," said the cat.

"Impossible," replied the Devil. "Even if it were possible to let people see you, you haven't been asked."

"That poses no problem."

"You can't just...*appear* on the float. Someone will notice."

"They'll all be too busy drinking bourbon and ogling tits to notice an extra rider. And those spangly masks cover one's face very well."

"But everyone will be able to see you're black. To this lot, that's far worse than being a cat."

"I'll shave," the cat decided. "My skin is actually a lightish gray. No one will suspect a thing."

The Devil was not overly optimistic about this scheme, but he had never once been able to stop the cat from doing whatever it wished. Indeed, it was better to indulge the creature. He went to the drugstore and bought twenty bottles of hair remover lotion. "No need for you to get a lot of nicks," he explained when he presented them to the cat.

"Nicks! Heh-heh! That's a good one, old boy. Don't worry so much. This parade will be one for the history books."

"That's what I'm afraid of," the Devil muttered unhappily. Contrary to his reputation, he was a rather cautious fellow, for evil often depends on maintaining the *status quo*.

Their house had a very large master bathroom completely tiled in black and white. In this cold and echoing chamber the Devil smoothed the foul-smelling hair remover lotion over the cat's body. Twenty minutes later, the cat stepped into the shower and emerged shuddering at the touch of the water, but completely hairless. His skin was light gray, as he had promised, and as smooth as a baby's. The Devil began to laugh.

"What's so funny?"

"Your head looks very small without its fur."

The cat looked in the mirror and tried to scowl, but his wrinkled little face looked so ridiculous that he couldn't help laughing too. They adjourned to the kitchen, took a bottle of vodka from the freezer, and spent the rest of the evening becoming quite drunk.

THE DEVIL YOU KNOW

✢

Lysander Byrne was the Captain of the Krewe of Onan, but everyone in New Orleans knew he didn't deserve the job. He'd made his money from Texas oil, then married Mignon Devore, the daughter of an old New Orleans family with Carnival roots that ran as deep as any in the city. When she was eighteen, Mignon had been Queen of Comus, and she still hung out her flag every year.

Mignon had maneuvered him into Onan, then arranged his rise to Captain, but he'd never been comfortable with it. Most of the men seemed to take the whole thing very seriously, as if the King's crown bestowed real royalty and the plastic beads they threw from their floats were truly jewels showered upon the peasantry. For Lysander, the whole thing was a giant exercise in humiliation.

He'd been embarrassed earlier this year by his son, Lysander Junior, otherwise known as Jay, who'd been recruited to escort a certain high-born girl to her debut. Jay hadn't shown up—Lysander suspected the boy had been drinking in the French Quarter, as he was prone to do—and of course the girl's family was furious. "It all reflects back on us," Mignon never tired of reminding him. Lysander sometimes considered pointing out the redundancy of the phrase *reflects back*, but he knew it would be pointless.

He was also worried about this new fellow who'd joined the krewe, who would in fact be riding on Lysander's float: one William Z. Bubb, known as Bill. The man made Lysander nervous for some reason, nothing he could pinpoint, just a feeling that the guy was somehow going to cause him further embarrassment. He'd had these feelings before and they were almost always accurate.

Lysander went upstairs and tapped on Mignon's bedroom door. She was in there "writing letters," her euphemism for her daily date with a bottle of blackberry brandy. If she wasn't too far gone, maybe he could talk to her about Mr. Bubb.

"Come in," she trilled. Lysander eased the door open. A small zephyr of scents wafted about him as he entered the room: powder, perfume, cigarettes, the sickly-sweet reek of the blackberry brandy.

"Minnie, hon, I wanted to ask you something about that new guy in Onan. Bill Bubb – "

"Oh, yes, isn't he just wonderful? He's a count, or a prince, or something fabulous like that—he's so modest, he didn't tell anyone, but Chrissy Saloom got it out of him."

"A count or a prince? From where?"

"Oh, somewhere in Europe."

"'Bubb' doesn't sound like a very European name."

"Don't be stupid, Ly. All names are European, unless they're African or Chinese or something like that."

He could see he would get nowhere with Mignon today; apparently she'd decided to celebrate the Carnival season by getting an early start on her daily date. He left her and went downstairs, where Jay was just coming in after having been gone all night. The boy looked wildly at Lysander as if seeing a stranger in the house. His pupils were enormous. His teeth seemed to be chattering. There was a smudge of blood on his shirt collar.

"Are you drunk too?" Lysander demanded.

"No, Dad, no way, jeez, I swear I haven't had a drink all night." Perhaps the boy was telling the truth; there was no smell of alcohol on him.

"Well, how about a cup of coffee, then?"

"Uh, no thanks, Dad, I'm pretty tired. I think I'll just go up to bed now." And Jay disappeared up the winding staircase, leaving Lysander alone once more.

The Onan parade rolled tonight, and the Devil was getting dressed. The now-bald cat stood behind him, where the Devil could just see him in the edge of the mirror. Each time the Devil donned a part of his brightly colored costume, the cat would produce an identical piece out of thin air and put it on his own lanky gray body.

"You're going to be caught," the Devil said. "They're not going to miss an extra rider, especially a giant gray one." The cat was almost seven feet tall when standing on his hind legs.

"They will not see me. I shall cloud their minds."

"You don't know how to do any such thing!"

"I've learned much from you," the cat replied, smiling.

The Devil swore, put the last touches to his costume, and slammed out of the house with a final warning he knew the cat would ignore. The truth was that he really didn't know what the cat could and could not do. In many ways it was more powerful than the Devil himself. Perhaps, if noticed, it would change into a bird and soar away, leaving the parade and its riders far below.

✢

Lysander was on the float, uncomfortable in his costume, attempting to untangle several hundred long strands of beads he intended to throw. Onan's theme this year was Mythical Creatures, and this float was decorated with several gauzy, iridescent, looming fairies. Their wings and gowns were lovely, but Lysander thought their avid papier-maché faces looked malevolent, more like those of witches than fairies.

The police escort arrived on time, the route was reported clear, and the parade began to roll without incident. Not until it had turned onto St. Charles and was rolling right past his house did Lysander look over at the new fellow. Standing right beside Mr. Bubb, hurling strands of faux pearls into the crowd with great abandon, was a completely unfamiliar figure. Of course, all the riders were masked, but anyone could tell that there was something strange about this character's face under the spangled hood. He looked almost like—Lysander could hardly credit it—a Negro!

Lysander was no racist; he often said as much to his friends and colleagues. He knew you weren't supposed to call them Negroes anymore, but no one could control what a man thought. He'd been raised to think of them as Negroes, if not something worse. And here was one riding on a float of Onan! It had never happened; it couldn't be happening now; but it was—and Lysander Byrne knew beyond a doubt that Mr.

Bubb had something to do with it. Yes, there he was, gesturing wildly at the unknown figure.

The parade ground to one of its frequent halts right in front of the Byrne house. Lysander saw Mignon sitting in their private viewing stand, staring straight at the masked Negro. Her expression was frozen.

When Lysander looked back at the float, the Negro had vanished. Could he have imagined seeing the man? He knew he had not imagined the look on Mignon's face. He was so shaken that he forgot to throw any beads for several blocks, despite the clamoring crowd.

✢

The majestic floats of Onan rolled one by one into the city auditorium. The parade was over, and the Devil was grateful. He'd noticed the Byrne man staring his way, looking utterly horrified. Surely the cat had been seen. Only at the last second had the two of them been able to avert disaster. Now came the ball, and the Devil would just have to brazen it out.

He had several drinks and danced several dances with lovely ladies, and he was just beginning to feel better when he saw Lysander Byrne approaching. The man looked like a walking heart attack, perspiring red face under his hood, great hanging gut barging through his green robe and pushing out the front of his purple tunic.

Byrne stopped in front of him, breathing heavily. "Did you enjoy the parade, Mr. Bubb?"

"Very much."

"Did you enjoy sneaking your friend onto our float? I don't know how you did it, but—"

"Sir, I assure you, there was no one with me."

"Dammit, I know I saw somebody. A Ne— a black fellow."

"I understood that blacks were not welcome in the Krewe of Onan," said the Devil.

Byrne cocked his head uncertainly. This was true, of course, but nobody ever said it right out loud.

"At any rate," the Devil said, "I've promised that young

lady over there a dance, so if you'll excuse me—"

"Hey! What's that under your robe?"

The Devil sighed. "I'm afraid you've caught me. I saw him in the gutter just before the parade began, and I couldn't bear to leave him lying there." He reached into his voluminous robe and pulled out a tiny gray kitten, completely hairless.

Lysander Byrne needed a drink in the worst way. He turned away from the Devil and pushed his way through the crowd to the bar. He did not look back. If he had, he would have seen the kitten grin, stretch its neck out to grotesque proportions, and take a big slug of the ice-cold vodka tonic in the Devil's hand.

In memory of Mikhail Bulgakov and John Kennedy Toole

O DEATH, WHERE IS THY SPATULA?

The main thing you need to know about me is that I love eating more than anything else in the world. More than sex, more than tropical vacations, more than reading, more than any drug I've ever tried. I'm not fat—I'm actually quite slender—but I can't take credit for any kind of willpower or exercise regimen. The truth is, I'm not fat because I only finish eating things that are really, really good, and there just aren't that many of them in my opinion. I love eating, as I say, but I'm picky as hell. A French pastry, ethereal manifestation of butter, custard, and chocolate, designed like a little piece of modern architecture? I'm there. A slice of cold pizza? I might nibble at it until my hunger headache goes away, but no more.

So, for the tale I'm about to relate, this food-love is the central fact of my being. I have a job (coroner of New Orleans), five purebred Oriental Shorthair cats, a mixed-breed husband (Irish and Jewish; wire-haired; his name is Reginald, but I never thought that suited him, so I call him Seymour), a house, and a hell of a lot of books, but none of that is terribly important here. What's important is that you understand how much I love to eat.

All right—the fact that I am the coroner of New Orleans is somewhat important too, but I don't want to put you off right away. Just store that information for future reference.

People think New Orleans is a world-class food city. Possibly it is, but only in a very narrow sense. There's a saying that we have a lot of great food but only about five recipes. Gumbo—etouffee—jambalaya—oysters Rockefeller—and I don't even know what the fifth one is supposed to be. Maybe breaded, deep-fried seafood, because we certainly have plenty of that. I see arteries full of it on my tables every day.

Perhaps I'm being unfair. There are, in fact, a lot of good restaurants here. But most of them…well, did you ever see that episode of *Frasier* where Frasier asks Niles, "What's the one thing better than a flawless meal?" and Niles answers, "A great meal with *one tiny flaw* we can pick at all night"? Most of the places here are like that, except the flaws aren't tiny. I can easily think of twenty places with excellent appetizers, terrific entrees, and dessert lists dull enough to plunge me into despair (apple tart, bread pudding, the eternal Death By Chocolate). There's a good French restaurant on Magazine Street where, even though I always pay with my credit card, the waiters refuse to acknowledge my existence—"May I clear that for you, sir?" they say, gazing lovingly at Seymour as they whisk away my salad plate. There's a simple neighborhood place where they used to have perfect fried chicken livers, but they hired a new fry cook, and now (no matter how I beg) the lovely little livers resemble nothing so much as deep-fried pencil erasers. I don't even want to talk about who and what you have to know to get a decent meal at the old-line venues like Antoine's.

There are problems everywhere. I eat at these restaurants anyway, and most of the time I enjoy them, but there is only one place where I know I can count on a flawless meal, without peer: Devlin Lemon's little restaurant in the Garden District. It's called the Lemon Tree and decorated with wrought iron baskets full of bright yellow lemons with their leaves still attached. In lesser hands it could have some serious cuteness issues. In Devlin's hands, you just want to prostrate yourself on the cerulean carpet and cry, "Feed me, you eponymous, lemon-stacking, brilliant fool." Or at least I do.

Devlin came from the frozen North with a Culinary Institute of America degree and a love for local ingredients. Anything that passes through his hands—a steak, a lobe of Hudson Valley foie gras, an unpasteurized French cheese—is likely to come out tasting good, but he has always reached the apex of his talent with Louisiana ingredients: Gulf fish, artichokes, Creole tomatoes, andouille and tasso, cane syrup, even mirlitons. I've never met another cook who could make a mirliton taste like anything but a sweaty sock. Devlin bakes them with shrimp, garlic, and a shocking amount of butter until they release a hitherto untold sweetness.

(All right, you nitpicking foodies. Yes, I am talking to you. I know you've been squirming since you read the words "unpasteurized French cheese," and I am quite aware that these ambrosial creations are legally forbidden to enter the country, let alone appear on a restaurant menu. The only thing I can say is all that's on the menu is not always all you can eat, and a good chef takes care of his regulars.)

Devlin knows everything I like and hate to eat. He knows that I am genetically disposed to think cilantro tastes like soap and that I can't stand cauliflower because it reminds me of certain cancers I see. He knows I will not eat amberjack under any circumstances; it was he who told me of the giant worms that lurk in its digestive tract. He knows how dearly I love sorrel, caviar, and clotted cream. At the Lemon Tree, I glance at the menu, but I usually end up telling my waitperson, "Ask Devlin what Dr. Brite should have today."

Lest you get the wrong idea, nothing has ever "happened," as they say, between us. We are both happily married. Any intimacy between me and Devlin is purely about his feeding and my eating.

It was May, close enough to my birthday that I had begun to wonder whether Devlin might find me something special—some Iranian caviar, perhaps, or some really fresh white truffles. I've never considered having my birthday dinner anywhere but the Lemon Tree, and some celebratory tidbit almost always finds its way onto the table.

I was at work in the basement of the big stone building at the corner of Tulane and Broad, where I spend a large part of my life. I'd spent the morning posting a young man killed in an automobile accident near the Calliope housing project (gross cranial trauma) and a fat old lady who died in her sleep (coronary event). I was beginning to think about lunch as my assistant wheeled out the last body that had come in the night before, a robbery victim who'd been shot in the head. I saw that the victim was wearing check-patterned chef's pants and work boots, but did not find this surprising. Kitchen workers keep strange hours and are often (wrongly) thought to be carrying large amounts of cash.

At first, I could only see that he was a young white man. The gun had been small and his cranium was intact, but even a low-caliber bullet to the head can distort facial features beyond recognition. This is mainly because the hemorrhaging of the brain produces gases that force blood into the tissues, particularly those around the eyes. This man's eyes were swollen shut and looked as if they had been smeared with heavy purple-black makeup. His lips were drawn rigidly across his teeth, and the teeth had dried blood on them. His hair was thickly crusted with blood; only a few clean strands told me that it had been strawberry-blonde. This may have been when the first breath of suspicion touched me, but if so, I did not notice it.

I parted the hair with my latex-gloved fingers. "Slightly stellate entry wound behind and below the right ear," I said to my assistant, Jeffrey, who wrote it down. "Stippling of the tissue around the entry wound. No exit wound. The bullet's still in there. What's his name?"

"That's a funny thing," said Jeffrey. "I can't find his report. I'm gonna have to call upstairs for the dupe."

"Well, go do it, please. I'll get him undressed." His shirt had already been removed. I picked up a pair of scissors and began to cut his pants off. As I did, his left hand slipped off the table and hung over the edge; rigor had not completely stiffened him yet.

Something about that hand caught my eye: a black ink

wedding band tattooed around the third finger. Many cooks don't like to wear wedding rings because they can so easily get snagged or lost, so this kind of tattoo is common. Devlin had one. His was done in a distinctive crosshatched pattern, just like the one on this man's hand.

I had opened one pants leg up to the crotch. Now I put the scissors down, moved to the head of the table, and looked carefully into the man's face. A warm rush of adrenaline spread through the muscles of my back as I saw what I had not seen before. The eyeball protrusion, tissue infiltration, and rigor had disguised him, but they could not hide his identity completely.

I was supporting my entire weight on the edge of the table when Jeffrey came back. "I don't have to call upstairs," he said. "I found his paperwork on the floor in the cooler—Dr. Brite? What's wrong?"

"I know him."

"Oh, hell."

"Let me see that paperwork." I scanned the police report, but it told me nothing I didn't already know: he had been shot in a robbery leaving the restaurant; he had been dead about eight hours; he was Devlin Lemon.

"I'm not posting him," I said.

"Well, of course not. We'll get Dr. Garrison to post him."

"*Nobody's* posting him," I said.

"What?"

"He can't—I mean, we can't—oh, God." I bowed my head to hide the tears that stood in my eyes. Jeffrey had never seen me cry. No one at the morgue had ever seen me cry. I don't socialize a great deal, but inevitably I had seen acquaintances on my tables before. I see everyone who dies in New Orleans. But none had affected me like this. I took a deep breath. "I have reason to suspect the presence of a communicable disease in this case," I said. It was the only half-plausible reason I could think of to delay the autopsy. "I'm keeping the body here until further notice."

"His family won't like that. Getty said they were already talking about holding a wake."

"I'll talk to them. I have no choice, Jeffrey. If there's a communicable disease involved, I can't release the body yet."

"Well, then, shouldn't we take fluids?"

"Later," I told him. "I need to...I need to read up on this. We may have to take special precautions."

Jeffrey's odd mint-green eyes met mine. He knew I was lying, and I knew that he knew. He trusted me, though; we worked well together. And he could see that I was rattled. He would drop the matter for now. "OK," he said. "Are you sure you don't want me to ask Dr. Garrison to speak with the family when he comes in?"

"No. I'll do it. I'll call them after lunch. I'm going to have lunch now."

I shut myself in my office just before the tears finally came. I curled up in my chair and hugged myself and cried. More than anything I wanted to call Seymour, but he and his brother were camping in Bogue Falaya for three days, unreachable.

Even if I could speak to Seymour, what would I say? I wasn't sure I could own up to what was in my head right now. I wasn't thinking of Devlin's family, or his youth, or the fear he must have felt when his murderer pressed the gun's muzzle against his skull. I wasn't thinking of Devlin at all, not exactly. I was thinking of the last appetizer I'd eaten at the Lemon Tree, a disk of beef marrow melting into a fricassee of chanterelles, its flavor brightened by a persillade so finely chopped you could barely see it. I was remembering the scent and savor of this dish. I could only remember it; I could not taste it, for the taste of loss was too bitter in my mouth.

When I finally washed my face and went back into the autopsy room, Devlin was gone. Jeffrey had zipped him into a body bag and rolled him back into the cooler. Maybe he'd feel comfortable there, I thought. Except for the presence of corpses, it was a lot like the walk-in refrigerator in a restaurant.

Was I losing my mind? It had been years since I thought that way about a dead person—as if he could feel comfortable, or feel pain, or have an opinion about his surroundings. Cutting open one body, sawing off the top of its skull, folding its face down and lifting the brain from its moorings had gone a long way toward convincing me that the dead do not care what is done to them. Doing these things thousands of times left me no doubt. I treat them with respect because they still matter to the living, but I no longer imagine them "feeling comfortable."

Now, though, I was.

I got through the rest of the day somehow. I even called Devlin's wife, whom I'd met once or twice at the restaurant. From the sound of her voice, I could tell she had been heavily tranquilized. She didn't argue when I told her I would have to keep Devlin's body for a few days. I expected to get a call from the wake-planning parents or siblings, but it didn't come. I left the morgue in the early evening, as twilight was falling over the city, and drove home. There I tried to eat some dry crackers, gagged on them, and crawled into bed with the cats.

A thin, sobbing, unearthly voice was trying to get me to hear it. "I'm hungry," it kept telling the darkness. "I'm hungry." It was trapped there, not knowing where it was or why. I tried to reply, but I could not form the words.

I wrenched myself awake, showered, and drove to the morgue hours before my next shift was scheduled to start. No one questioned my presence: they left me alone, assuming I had work to catch up on—which I did, in a way. I wheeled Devlin out of the cooler and slid him onto one of the tables, my back muscles knotting in protest. I ignored the pain. After measuring and photographing the bullet wound in his skull, I washed away the blood, used a disposable plastic razor to shave the hair around the area, and inserted a pair of long forceps into the hole. I was afraid that the bullet had ricocheted inside his skull, hiding itself among scrambled pieces of brain, but my forceps traveled a straight track to the region of his cerebellum and found metal. I pulled out a bloody bit of lead with a slightly flattened tip. I caught myself thanking God, or somebody, for my findings—his brain was not destroyed; the bullet had not shattered into fragments I would have to search out. What was I thinking? It didn't matter how little damage had been done. Devlin was still dead.

I wondered what was happening to me as I triple-bagged the bullet, put it in a padded envelope, and left the building with it tucked under my arm. I might not lose my job if anyone found out about this, but only because I am a good liar and could probably come up with a plausible reason for my actions. In truth, I didn't know what I was doing or why.

Usually Seymour brings me my coffee in bed, and I drink it with plenty of milk and sugar. This morning I drank it black in a Styrofoam cup from a gas station. Then I drove to the French Quarter, parked on Royal Street, and walked to St. Louis Cathedral. I was not raised Catholic, but I'd lit candles here to ask for various small favors, and they had all been granted. I lit a candle now, stuffing a ten-dollar bill into the collection box, looking into the porcelain faces of Mary and her small son. Then I slid into a pew and sat there for a long time.

I did not pray, exactly. I didn't know how. Instead I thought of marrow melting into chanterelles, of whole roasted snapper with wild-rice-stuffed figs, of fresh sweet Gulf shrimp on a bed of crisp fried spinach. I tried to remember everything Devlin had ever cooked for me, and as I did so, I slid my hand into the padded envelope and clutched the bullet in its triple layer of plastic.

I felt a little better when I came out of the cathedral. By noon, Jackson Square would be full of tacky fortunetellers, bad musicians, and ugly tourists, but right now it was peaceful. My good mood lasted until I went back to work, looked in the cooler, and saw Devlin there. His face had begun to look haggard from dehydration, and the bullet that had been in his head was now in its padded envelope under the front seat of my car. Nothing else had changed. I don't know what I expected. If prayers could cause the dead to get up and walk away, I would have been out of work long ago.

"You look sick," said Jeffrey. "I swear you've lost weight since yesterday."

"Thanks."

"Why don't you go home? Dix and I can handle things here."

"I'm fine," I said. But after lunch—which I could not eat—I felt worse than ever. "Do you really think you and Dix would be all right if I went home?" I asked Jeffrey.

"Absolutely. Get out of here and get some rest. And some food," he called after me. "Get yourself a hot meal."

"I'm trying," I muttered as I got into my car. Though it was only April, temperatures were already in the eighties, and I wondered if I was really picking up the dark rich smell of the blood on the bullet under my seat.

I did not go straight to my destination. Instead I stopped at a nice restaurant on St. Charles Avenue and attempted to have lunch. There was nothing wrong with any of the food I ordered, but it all seemed to taste of ashes and decay. The waiter wanted to know if there was a problem. I said I'd had the flu and would take the leftovers with me, and he encased them in a foil swan, which I threw away as soon as I left the place. In two days I had managed to eat perhaps two grams of food. It was time to seek serious help.

I knew enough to stay out of the Quarter this time. The places that billed themselves as voodoo shops there were tourist traps, pure and simple. But I didn't know where to go. I had noticed a building on Broad Street, near my workplace, with words like CANDLES and HERBS and BOTANICA painted on its side. The woman behind the counter had skin the shade and texture of a Brazil nut. Her eyes were gorgeous: large and tilted, fringed with dark lashes, the irises a color somewhere between green and gold.

"Can I help you?" she asked, and I stood there stupidly. I had finally admitted to myself what I wanted to do, and in the same breath I had realized that there was no sane way to ask for it. I didn't particularly care whether I sounded sane, but if I asked how to raise the dead, the woman would probably throw me out of her shop.

I didn't know what I was going to say until I heard myself saying it. "I'm a writer," I said, and almost laughed. I *had* kidded myself that my ramblings had literary merit, once upon a time, but those days were long gone. "I'm writing a story in which someone wants to bring a corpse back to life. Like they're supposed to do in Haiti. Do you have any information on that?"

Those devastating eyes regarded me levelly. "Of course," she said. "There are books. Of course, the dead can't actually return to life—you understand that?" Perhaps my voice was a little too ragged, the skin around my eyes a little too red—but couldn't these be side effects of late writing hours?

"It's only a story," I told her.

"Good." She took a book from a shelf near the counter. Its black cover was embossed with a single word, **VODOUN**. "The recipe is on page fifty-three. You'll recognize most of the ingredients—in fact, you'll find most of them in your kitchen. But you may not have heard of datura, also known as the zombi cucumber."

"What's that?"

"A powerful hallucinogen, among other things." She took down another book, this one titled *Plants of the Gods*. "You can learn more about it in here."

"Where can I, uh, where can my characters get it?"

"You can't. Not unless you grow it yourself, or find it growing wild—it's illegal." Her eyes shone, and I wondered if she thought she was saving me from something.

"Then it won't work," I said. I have killed every plant I ever tried to grow, and the idea of tramping around some wilderness trying to identify a hallucinogenic plant was just silly—I can't even stand to go camping with Seymour and his brother.

Nonetheless, I paid for both books, took them home, and spread them out on my desk. As the woman had promised, most of the ingredients in the voodoo (or vodoun) spell were familiar, but it was obvious that datura was central to the thing. This seemed like an insurmountable obstacle at first. Then I turned to the entry for datura in *Plants of the Gods*, and I began to wonder.

The book told me that datura grows in tropical and temperate zones in both hemispheres, and that all species have tropane alkaloids as their active principles. Organic chemistry was the only part of medical school that I found nearly impossible to get through, and I had studied it so hard that I still remembered most of it. Even if I hadn't, the names of three tropane alkaloids were listed in the book: atropine, hyoscyamine, and scopolamine. I handled at least two of these compounds on a weekly basis.

When a person dies at home, any medications he or she is

taking are supposed to be brought into the morgue with the body. We note these medications on the autopsy report, count the pills, and (at least in theory) wash them down the sink. Atropine is the active ingredient in Lomotil, which is used to control severe diarrhea. Hyoscyamine is used in Cystospaz and Uriced, which are used for glaucoma, urinary obstructions, and bowel problems. These three drugs come in with bodies all the time; I was certain that there were some waiting to be counted in the morgue right now. Scopolamine is used in transdermal motion-sickness patches, which I don't see as often, but it would be easy to get one.

I wrote myself a prescription for a scopolamine patch and drove to a Walgreen's to fill it. I could write myself scripts for the others, too, but Lomotil is a controlled substance. I didn't want somebody recognizing my name and spreading rumors. I'd see if the drugs were available at the morgue. If not, the Walgreen's was open all night.

I could hardly make myself wait until midnight, but there was no way I could do anything at the morgue before then; too many people would be there. I gathered the other ingredients I needed and tried to make myself take a nap, but hunger pangs kept me awake. I fed the cats. I read more of the **VODOUN** book and learned that I was taking an enormous risk, not with Devlin, but with my own soul. I was tampering with the fabric of reality and would eventually have to pay a price. I didn't care. With Devlin dead, I thought I might never be able to eat again, so I would soon be dead too.

When midnight came, I forced myself to wait another half-hour. Then I packed up the things I needed and drove to work.

I had been afraid that a traffic accident or a house fire would have caused a spate of activity, but everything was quiet; only the night assistant and the janitor were there. Even so, I wheeled Devlin into the decomp room. He hadn't begun to decompose, but that room could be locked and there was no window in the door.

First I sewed up the skin over his head wound. I realized I should have done this earlier, as the skin had begun to curl and shrink away from the edges of the wound, but I did as well as I could. I had already cleaned the area around the wound, but now I washed all the blood from his hair, head, and neck. I didn't know what had happened to his shirt, so I had brought in the top of a green scrub suit. Rigor mortis had passed and his limbs moved easily, but I was not strong enough to wrestle him into the top. I put it on an instrument tray nearby.

Finding the Lomotil, Cystospaz, and Uriced had been no problem. I crushed the pills, cut the scopolamine patch into tiny pieces, and mixed them with most of the other ingredients in an organ-specimen jar. The copy of **VODOUN** was open to page fifty-three on the counter, and I checked the recipe to make sure I had done everything right. I had only the last two steps to go.

"The final ingredient," the text read, "is a finger bone taken from a living person."

I sterilized my hands, my bone saw, and a heavy kitchen cleaver I'd brought from home. I had been tempted to grab a couple of painkillers along with the other pills, but I was afraid they would make me groggy. I had to be absolutely aware of what I was doing. I splayed my left hand on the steel table, expelled a long breath, and brought the cleaver down on the first joint of my forefinger.

This may seem senseless. The spell did not specify which finger to use, and I rely on my hands for my livelihood; why didn't I choose my relatively useless pinky finger? I'm not sure. I was doing what I felt I had to do—had been from the moment I first saw Devlin on my table, really—and all I can say is that my pinky didn't feel important enough. I didn't know how the spell would work, if it did work, but I understood that the finger bone had to be taken from a living person because it was a sacrifice.

I didn't need the bone saw at all. The cleaver went through the flesh, through the bone, and the joint skittered across the table's slick surface. It would have fallen to the floor if the table hadn't had a raised lip for catching blood and other fluids. I only looked at my left hand long enough to sink a few clumsy stitches into the raw flesh and slap on a butterfly bandage. The stitches were the most painful part of the whole procedure. When I had stopped the bleeding, I turned my attention to the severed joint. The book didn't say anything about meat, blood, or nerves: it said a finger *bone*, so I used a scalpel to dissect away as much of the other material as I could before dropping the slick little bone into the jar of ingredients.

As I mixed everything together, I felt ravenous. Hunger, exhaustion, and shock were preying on me now; I think I believed Devlin was going to get off that table and immediately fix me a nice meal.

It was ready. I had done everything else; there was only the last step to go. I tilted Devlin's head back, pulled his lower jaw down, and poured the mixture into his mouth.

Nothing happened.

Maybe the mixture had to dissolve, I thought. It wouldn't do so on its own because his mouth was so dried out. I ran some water into the jar and let it trickle between his lips.

Still nothing.

"Goddamn it," I said. "Devlin, you fucking asshole, *come back here!*"

I guess that was why the title of the recipe was "Calling Back the Dead." You had to actually call them. Because as soon as I spoke, Devlin opened his eyes.

I had the scalpel in my hand, not so much because I was afraid of him as because I was afraid for him. The book didn't say anything about what the person would be like when they came back. I didn't want a zombie, didn't want him in some mindless state of animated limbo. That would be worse than staying dead—and I doubted very much whether a zombie knew enough to hold a haunch of meat over a fire, let alone make a foie gras crème brulee. If he was merely animated—if *Devlin himself* wasn't there—I was prepared to drive the scalpel into the base of his skull, doing essentially what the bullet had done before. I don't know what I thought I would do if that didn't work.

But I never had to worry about it, because as soon as he opened his eyes, I saw the man I knew in them. And as soon as his eyes met mine, he said, "Dr. Brite?"

Then the mixture hit the back of his throat and he began

to cough. Wouldn't that have been cute, if I'd brought him back to life only to have him choke on my severed finger bone? "Devlin," I said, "*swallow*." He did, and the obstruction went down.

"I feel terrible," he said.

"We need to get you to a hospital."

"Where are we? What happened?"

"You've been hurt. There was a terrible mistake, but it's going to be all right."

And it was. There were questions, of course, but I stuck to my story that I'd found Devlin exhibiting vital signs after two days of refrigeration. It was highly unlikely but impossible to disprove, especially with the man sitting there, breathing and talking. Nobody ever connected my missing finger joint with Devlin's resurrection. I just said I'd had an accident while cutting meat, which was essentially true. Seymour may have been a little suspicious of this story, since he would have expected me to save the severed joint in formalin as a souvenir, but he must have seen that I was in an odd mood when he returned from his camping trip; he asked very few questions.

Devlin didn't remember anything after leaving the Lemon Tree the night of the robbery. The version of reality that most people came to accept—because any other version simply stretched the mind beyond its capacity—was that the bullet had not penetrated Devlin's skull at all, but had worked like a hard blow to the head, rendering him unconscious for a protracted period.

Only Jeffrey knew otherwise. He saw Devlin's body up close. He knows very well what a dead person looks like, and he knows me. But he has never said a word. That's one reason he is my favorite assistant.

For my birthday dinner, I had a Creole tomato aspic with lump crabmeat and sorrel, a dozen Kumamoto oysters topped with sevruga caviar, a plate of braised veal cheeks so tender they dissolved in my mouth, and a miniature heart-shaped chocolate cake with a chocolate sphere full of raspberry puree somehow concealed in the middle. The last item in particular made me think Devlin knew I had done something more than find him warm on the autopsy table. Like Jeffrey, though, he never said anything. He didn't have to. He continues to feed me all the thanks I need.

LANTERN MARSH

The marsh brooded on the outskirts of town. We children sometimes played there during the day, poling flat-bottomed boats through the dark water choked with swamp hyacinth, stranding ourselves on any of the hundreds of tiny islands. By day the marsh was a place of filtering, shifting patches of sunlight, cypress and live oak bearded with Spanish moss, velvety brown cattails that would burst into clouds of white snow if you smacked them against the back of your friend's head, and unfounded rumors of quicksand pools full of skeletons and treasure.

At night, the lanterns took over.

Our parents forbade us to go into the marsh at night. Usually this rule needed no enforcing, but at one time or another, most of us had worked up enough courage to creep to the edge of the marsh with a group of friends, stare for a while at the bright globes of light hovering over the water, and then run away as fast as our legs could carry us. Later we would laugh and call one another fraidy-cat, but not until we were back home in somebody's warm, well-lit room. After all, no one really knew what the lanterns were—our science teachers dismissed them as swamp gas, but hardly anybody believed that—or what they could do, if in fact they wanted to do anything besides hover and shimmer, be beautiful luminous ghosts.

We had lived in the town named after this marsh all our lives.

+

Our first encounter with Mr. Prudhomme—and the first indication I had that Noel was perhaps not entirely sane about the marsh—took place on a Halloween afternoon when we (Noel, Bronwen, and me, Phil) were all ten years old. School had let out early that day. By some obscure tradition, Halloween in Lantern Marsh had always been a big occasion for the kids—maybe just because there wasn't really much for us to do the rest of the year—so the schools scheduled a half-day or canceled altogether.

The three of us were walking down the town's main street, enjoying the tangy autumn flavor of the air. This was the Deep South and Halloween often felt more like August, but this year we were having a decent cool season. Bronwen and I were talking about the costumes we were going to wear that night. Noel, who never went trick-or-treating, walked silently along beside us, hands shoved in pockets, thinking his private thoughts.

Suddenly he stopped in his tracks and stared across the street. "Look—look—there he is!"

We were used to Noel's intense reactions, but this time we had no idea what he might be reacting to. "Who?" I asked.

Noel jerked his head toward a shop door on the other side of the street, where a tall red-haired man stood talking to the shopkeeper. "That's George Prudhomme, the guy who runs that building company—Marshwood Development. He's a fucking bastard."

"Noel!" said Bronwen.

"Well, he *is*! He owns half the land the marsh is on. Last

year, right after Halloween, he told my mother I'd been trespassing on his land. I didn't even go into the marsh, I was just watching the lanterns like I always do, but she bawled me out anyway. This year I told her I was going out trick-or-treating with you guys."

Noel had lived with his mother for seven years, ever since his father left for parts unknown. She was a big, ruddy woman who always smelled of cigarettes, and she frightened me and Bronwen a little, but she and Noel had negotiated an uneasy peace.

"Why *don't* you come out with us?" I said. "Seems like that'd be a lot more fun that watching those old lanterns again." Although I knew the lanterns were magic to Noel, I couldn't conceive of not wanting to go trick-or-treating. The idea of coming home at the end of the night empty-handed, with no laden plastic bag into which you could stick your face and breathe the odor of all kinds of candy mingling...

But Noel just shook his head.

Bronwen tucked a scrap of yellow hair behind her ear as she looked across the street at Prudhomme. "That man wants to hurt you, Noel."

I looked at her, puzzled. Why had she said that? But the red-haired man was beckoning to Noel. Bronwen clutched Noel's arm. "Don't go!"

"It's OK, Bron. He can't hurt me here."

Noel crossed the street and stood in front of the big man, fists on hips, dark shaggy head thrown back, looking ridiculously small. Prudhomme said something to him, and Noel shook his head *no*. After a moment or two, Bronwen and I relaxed—it looked like they were just going to have a conversation after all. But then Noel began to shout.

"You can't do it, you dirty *shit*! I know you can't because you only own half of it! And if you ever try, I...I'll kill you! I swear I will!" Prudhomme stared obliquely down at him. When Noel turned and ran back to us, I saw that his features were contorted with rage, close to tears. Without waiting to see whether we would follow, he started off down the street, his back held stiff and straight. We hurried after him, not knowing what else to do.

When we caught up with him, all three of us strode along in silence for several minutes. Then Bronwen, always the peacemaker, touched Noel's shoulder and asked, "What did he say?"

Noel scowled. "He told me to stay away from the marsh tonight, like he always does if he sees me around Halloween. But I don't care what he says. He'll never know—he's too scared to go near the marsh on Halloween night. And he ought to be scared, too, because I bet they hate him as much as I do."

They? He meant the lanterns, I realized. Though I knew how they obsessed him, I'd never known that he believed they could love or hate.

But this realization was overshadowed by another. "That's not what made you so mad," I said.

Noel gazed at me. The expression on his face now was more fear than fury. "He said—he said someday he was going to fill in the marsh!" His lips trembled and he bit at them, swallowing hard. Finally he cried.

And well he might, for Noel had lived at the edge of the marsh all his life. His house was closer to it than any other in town. Ever since Bronwen and I had made friends with him in the first grade, we had been familiar with his fierce hatreds and equally fierce loves, his wild plans that always seemed to work, the mixture of sadness and rage that always seemed to linger just below the surface of his eyes…and his utter refusal to go trick-or-treating on Halloween night. Instead he would sit for hours at the edge of the water and watch the lanterns as if they were his own personal light show. On Halloween, he claimed, they were at their most spectacular. Spirits could visit the living world on Halloween, and Noel had always thought the lanterns were spirits. There were hundreds of the great glowing balls, and more mirrored in the dark water. They darted and showered sparks and made the whole marsh glow, and most of us had grandparents or other older relatives who'd assured us that anyone foolish enough to go into the marsh on the spirits' night wouldn't come out again. Noel brushed off all these warnings. He didn't go into the marsh on Halloween; he only wanted to watch. He was never able to explain this to the satisfaction of me and Bronwen, who loved our conventional, costumed Halloween as much as any other kids. It took us a few years to realize that Halloween was a time of magic for Noel too, magic far more potent than ours.

After the night's adventures, we crept to the edge of the marsh with the taste of candy in our mouths and the smell of burning pumpkinflesh still trailing behind us. Bronwen was a yellow-haired gypsy rattling loads of costume jewelry. I was a black-masked bandit marred by my mother's strips of orange reflecting tape. We would never have gone alone to the marsh on Halloween night, but knowing that Noel would be there, we felt protected somehow.

"Noel?" I whispered into the darkness.

Something white rose up behind a tree. Bronwen gave a little shriek, but the flapping shape said "Ssssst!" and waved us over. When we got to him, I saw that Noel was in costume, presumably to fool his mother. He was dressed all in white, with white smudges of makeup smudged around his dark, dark eyes. If the spookiness of the marsh itself hadn't scared off any intruders, Noel might have.

Bronwen held out an extra bag heavy with candy corn and miniature chocolate bars. "We brought you some."

Noel accepted the bag like a prince and gave us one of his rare smiles. "Thanks." He considered us for a moment and apparently found us worthy. "Do you want to see them?" I hesitated, but Bronwen nodded.

Noel led us to his spot behind the tree. I looked into the depths of the marsh and saw nothing. Bronwen glanced off to the left and said "*Oh!*", enthralled. For there they were, the hovering, darting colored globes. They drew closer as we watched. Depthless black water reflected them back a hundred times over, rippling and shimmering. Their pale light spilled between the trees, bathing our faces; tiny lanterns danced in Noel's eyes. For the first time I knew that he wanted to join them, whatever the price of that joining might be. But he had always been adamant about looking after his mother, who would be alone without him. For now, at least, he would have to content himself with these nighttime glimpses.

We watched the lanterns dance for what felt like hours, until I heard my mother calling me home from blocks away.

✦

Eventually Bronwen and I graduated from trick-or-treating to costume parties at our friends' houses. Noel, though, still spent his rapt nights at the edge of the marsh each Halloween. He and George Prudhomme glared at each other when they met in the drugstore or the Central Park Café, but as far as I knew, no more words passed between them. We moved up from elementary school to the county consolidated junior high, where Noel's strangeness was judged less acceptable by kids who hadn't known him most of his life. Noel refused to even try to act normal, and so he was tormented. "The three C's of adolescence," he said to us more than once, "clothes, cliques, and cruelty." But he answered the teasing with sarcasm or indifference. Being ignored only made his tormentors angrier, and if he had to, Noel would fight. He usually won, too. Noel was skinny but wiry, and he clawed at his opponents with a mad abandon that usually kept them from challenging him twice.

By the time we got to high school, most people left Noel alone. He would never be accepted, but acceptance wasn't something he needed. More and more often, instead of going to the pep club meetings or basketball games that had captivated us earlier in our teens, Bronwen and I would join Noel in his room after school to listen to the Beatles, the Doors, Jimi Hendrix. We were learning that we didn't need acceptance either.

The three of us, now as close again as we had been in childhood, decided to form a band. Bronwen could play the guitar a little, and I began to get interested in drumming, something I'd previously practiced on the edges of desks and dinner tables. My parents bought me a used set, good enough to start out on, for fifty dollars. Noel needed no instrument. He had a high wail of a singing voice, huge and soulful and strangely beautiful. Our name, of course, was the Lanterns. We played at a couple of school dances, doing mostly Beatles and Stones covers but also a few songs Noel had written himself. We weren't well-received by the dance crowds, and after our first two gigs we were replaced by another garage band that played fifties hits and beach music. Noel didn't care. He had never been concerned about performing in public anyway, especially to a high school audience; he had only agreed to it because the idea excited me and Bronwen.

We didn't play any more gigs, but the Lanterns lasted through the summer after our high school graduation. Then Bronwen and I went to the state university, and Noel, who was planning to major in music, went to a small liberal arts college about a hundred miles away from Lantern Marsh. His mother wasn't happy to see him go, but as he had received a full scholarship, she could do nothing to stop him. At the state school, Bronwen and I met crowds of new people, but we always came back to each other. Noel wrote us long letters about learning to play guitar and piano (which he liked) and the atmosphere at his college, elite and self-consciously eccentric (which he claimed to dislike, but even he had to admit it beat high school). I bought a secondhand green Volkswagen Bug. Bronwen got her ears pierced. Things went smoothly until our fall break, when we were pleased to find out that Noel would be coming home at the same time we would.

Driving home, I gave half my attention to Bronwen and half to worrying about my bald tires. My parents had offered to replace them while I was home, but I wasn't even sure they would last out the trip. As we approached Lantern Marsh, my worry was interrupted. Bronwen gasped and craned forward in her seat. "Phil—look!"

We were entering town by a road that went past a far edge of the marsh. The marsh was still there, of course; but it was changed, weakened. Instead of a line of cypress and oak, I saw stumps, red mud, bulldozers and dump trucks. A large patch of land had been filled and cleared. A billboard announced in foot-high red letters:

FUTURE SITE OF
MARSHWOOD MALL
A PROPERTY OF MARSHWOOD DEVELOPMENT

At home, my father confirmed my fears. "George Prudhomme bought the rest of the marsh. Shame to tear it up if you ask me, but it wasn't making the town any money. People say he's having the whole thing filled in to build a new shopping center with a double-decker parking lot. You used to have a friend who liked the marsh, didn't you, Phil?"

When I called Noel's house, his mother said he wouldn't be home until the next day. Her voice on the phone was little more than a faint wheeze, and I wondered if she was thinking of what Prudhomme's plans might do to her son. Bronwen had gone out to dinner at the Three Lanterns Steakhouse with her family. My mom had fixed a welcome-home meal of pork chops, mashed potatoes, and strawberry shortcake, all my favorites. I wasn't able to enjoy it much. My parents could tell I was worried, but they thought it must have something to do with school. Of course I wasn't thinking about school at all. I was wondering what in the world we were going to say to Noel tomorrow, and whether it would do any good.

As it turned out, we didn't have to break the news to him. His bus had come into town by the same road we'd used, so he already knew. His mother looked awful when she let us in. She'd always been a fleshy woman, and still was, but now the flesh seemed to sag off her bones. Her color was high and unhealthy-looking, as if she'd been running a fever. "He's in his room," she told us. "Hasn't hardly been out since he got here."

Bronwen knocked on the door. "Come in," said Noel hollowly.

He was sitting in the dark. Well, not quite; he had put his red light bulb in the bedside lamp. It cast a bloody glow over the room but offered little illumination. Noel's eyes were nothing but dark hollows in his angular face.

"What are you going to do?" Bronwen asked, putting her hand on his arm.

"Kill Prudhomme," he said without fervor. "Nine years ago I told him I'd kill him if he ever tried this. Now I've got to do it."

This made me impatient. "Come on, Noel. You can't kill

Prudhomme. What would you accomplish? You'd go to jail and the mall would get built anyway."

Noel nodded. I wasn't sure if he'd heard me, but he already knew the truth of what I said. He stared at a poster on the wall behind Bronwen and me, Jim Morrison in his Lizard King pose. "What am I going to do, you ask? I'm going to sit here and watch Prudhomme tear up the marsh. Maybe they'll be able to stop him, maybe not. If I could join them, I'd damn well stop him."

"You mean the lanterns?" Bronwen asked timidly. But we all knew what he meant. Noel had always wanted to join the lanterns, to become one with them, but his mother would be alone in the world without him. Now I wondered if even that would be enough to keep him here.

He lay back on his bed. "Listen, I need to think. Can you leave me alone for a while?" We nodded and left silently. It was the first time Noel had ever sent us away.

The next afternoon, as I was leaving the house, my father stopped me with a stricken look on his face. "Have you talked to your friend Noel?"

"Not today, but I was just going over there."

"You won't find him at his house."

"Why not?"

Dad sighed. "Phil, Noel's mother died last night. She had a stroke, was gone right away. Noel called 911, but when the ambulance got there, they couldn't find him. No one's seen the boy since."

A thought nudged me. With exams right before the break, I'd lost track of dates... "What day is this?"

"The thirty-first," my father said, and I couldn't believe I'd forgotten.

"BRONWEN!" I yelled, still half a block away and glimpsing her yellow hair through the foliage that masked her front porch. Soon we were running toward the marsh where it came closest to Noel's house. We hunted up one of the flat-bottomed boats we hadn't used since we were twelve or so. Awkwardly, too heavy for the boats, we poled through the edges of the marsh calling Noel's name. He could be anywhere, but I wanted to find him before nightfall. Because now, with his mother gone, there was nothing to hold him here.

It felt as though we covered miles of the marsh, sometimes poling and sometimes just letting the boat drift, starting with hope at every bird-sound and frog-ripple. As the sky between the trees deepened into twilight, our courage failed. We dragged the boat back up onto solid ground behind Noel's house. Blocks away, we heard the shouts of early trick-or-treaters.

Something white rose up behind a tree.

"I came to say goodbye," said Noel. As he had been years ago, he was dressed all in white. There were no theatrical smudges of makeup around his eyes this time, just dark circles of exhaustion. He'd been up all night, I could tell. "I knew you'd come here, but I can't stay long. I couldn't go without saying goodbye."

"Don't go," I said.

"You know I have to."

He leaned toward Bronwen and kissed her lips. Then he turned to me, and I hugged him as hard as I could. I might have been able to hold him back at that moment, but I didn't try. I let him go. "Goodbye, Bron…Phil," he whispered, and his voice broke just a little on my name. Then he stepped into our little boat and, standing easily, pushed himself away from the land. He was far better at it than we had been, shifting his weight with the water. He knew this marsh so well.

Soon the boat was invisible through the moss-fringed trees; we could just make out the white form of Noel guiding it between the shadowy hummocks of grass. The lanterns flickered in the distance. We could tell when Noel reached them, because they began to dance. Their colors grew brighter, as if disturbed at the intruder in their midst. Bronwen's hand tightened on my arm, and I covered it with my own.

Noel began to sing to the lanterns.

At first his voice reached us like a thread of leftover summer breeze, faint but sweet. Then it grew stronger, and though I couldn't make out the words, I knew Noel had penned them himself. His voice was hoarse and high, more gorgeous than ever. In it was the Arcadian splendor of the marsh and its spookiness, the joy it had brought him and the anguish he felt at losing it, the pure golden glory of the lanterns themselves. It was a tribute and a plea. We could see his tiny form in the distance, the lanterns surrounding him, weaving around him, dancing to Noel's song. "Now! Now! NOW..." I heard him shriek, and the lanterns suddenly grew brighter than we had ever seen them, so bright we could not look at them. We turned away, shielding our eyes from what might have been a small supernova in the heart of the marsh. When we looked back, the blinding light had vanished. Noel and the lanterns were gone.

No one in town expected to see Noel again. They figured he'd either gone back to his arty school or drowned in the fabled quicksand of the marsh on Halloween night, and no one outside of our tiny circle much cared. But a week later, just before Bronwen and I were due back at school, Lantern Marsh discovered that one of its more solid citizens had gone missing. The police wouldn't do anything for twenty-four hours, so Marshwood Development organized its own search party; rumor had it that things hadn't been going well at the company, and perhaps they were nervous. They had reason. Before the day was out they found George Prudhomme hanged from the heavy limb of an oak tree in the middle of the marsh, his thick neck stretched by hemp, his red hair shivering in the wind.

Some tried to call it murder and blame it on vanished Noel; there were plenty who recalled his hatred of the man. But his foreman at the company said Prudhomme had refused to go into the marsh for days, and the pharmacist revealed that he'd filled a prescription of strong sleeping pills for Prudhomme. General consensus was that the man had been afraid of something.

And who could they blame for the bulldozer whose engine suffered irreparable, impossible rust damage overnight? Or the fire that broke out at the office of Marshwood Development, nearly killing a file clerk? Prudhomme's vice president told the local newspaper, "We're superstitious, but we're not stupid either. Marshwood

Development has sold the entire parcel of land to the federal government to be turned into a wildlife sanctuary. It's a beauty of a tax writeoff." My father, an accountant at the paper, told us the man had actually said "a wet dream of a tax writeoff," and my mother nearly choked with laughter at the dinner table.

As for me and Bronwen—well, on the night before we had to return to school, we took a walk along the deserted main street of the town. We passed the doorway where Noel had shouted at Prudhomme, the drugstore where we had read horror comics and eaten ice cream, the school where Noel had taken his torment like a Stoic. We deliberately avoided Noel's empty house and the marsh near it. But as we were about to turn down the street that would return us home, Bronwen stopped and tilted her head. "Listen," she said.

We both listened. We stood together on the dark street corner and listened for a long time, until a cold wind began to run its fingers under our collars. Bronwen shivered and tucked her arm under mine. We went on our way, not speaking of what we had heard on the corner.

Far away, from the direction of the marsh, we had heard faint strains of eerie, lovely music.

NOTHING OF HIM THAT DOTH FADE

The two Americans surfaced slowly, dizzy from the sights of the Great Barrier Reef: the endless billowing vistas of coral, the lone, shy, deadly blue-ringer octopus, the crown-of-thorns starfish that was beautiful even as it gradually nibbled away the reef. The boat was nowhere in sight. They removed their mouthpieces, cleared their face masks of water, and looked again. The boat was still gone.

"I think they've left us," said Theo.

"Don't be stupid," said Jack.

They had arrived in Australia a week and a half ago, starting out in gay-friendly Sydney to acclimatize themselves and avoid hearing, at least for a few days, the ago-old but tiresome question *Are you two ... together*? Neither of them wanted to answer that, not about each other, not any more.

Both were in their late thirties. Theo, a pastry chef, was

broad across the shoulders, handsome in the manner of an aging schoolboy, conciliatory unless his patience was stretched too far. Jack, a freelance writer for magazines, was long and lean, hatchet-faced and red-headed, always ready with a side-of-the-mouth barb to stretch Theo's patience. They had spent twelve years in each other's company. The first eight or so had been good. The trip was an attempt to recapture the goodness. In his heart, neither believed it would work, but the idea of having again what they'd once taken for granted was worth the time, money, and chance.

It was impossible to put one's finger on the moment when things had begun to go sour between them. They'd never been one of those couples who got along perfectly, or seemed to: even during the first couple of years their fights were frequent, loud, and passionate. Sometimes they reconciled with furious lovemaking. More often they would wake up the next morning and find that the whole thing just seemed silly. They were friends as well as lovers then. Friends could fight, air it out, then put it behind them. Friends could laugh at such things; they had spent much time laughing together.

It was when they stopped fighting that things had begun to atrophy. Now, instead of fighting, they sniped constantly. A shortcoming pointed out here, an old grievance dredged up there. It was a habit that clung as closely to them as they had once clung to each other. Friends did not snipe. But Jack and Theo were no longer friends.

The Sydney harbor threw off azure sparkles. The famous silhouette of the opera house rose above the water like the tail flukes of a white whale diving deep. Jack and Theo chose an outdoor table at a café that promised harbor-caught seafood.

"It's too windy out here," Jack said after a few minutes, weighing down his flapping paper napkin with his knife.

"It feels good. Smells like the ocean."

"Fine." Jack pulled his windbreaker tightly around his lanky frame and huddled into himself.

"Let's go inside," Theo said after a few minutes.

"No, it's fine, you wanted to stay out here."

"You're cold. You're making that quite obvious. We won't be able to enjoy our lunch. Come on, let's go in."

"Don't worry about it."

Theo rose from the table, grabbing his napkin and silverware. "I said let's go in the fucking restaurant!" He turned and stalked through the double doors of the café, not turning to see if Jack followed. After a minute, Jack did.

The combination platter of prawns, oysters, and Balmain bugs was fresh and delicious. Ten minutes after it was served, Theo started checking his watch.

"What's wrong?" Jack asked.

"The food took so long to come—if we don't get going soon, we'll miss the one-fifteen ferry over to the zoo."

"So we'll catch the next one."

"I wanted to get there by two o'clock."

"What difference does it make?"

"It's a big zoo. We won't have time to see it all if we don't get there early enough."

"So we'll see whatever we have time for."

"What's the point of that? If we're not going to see it all, we may as well not go. In fact, let's just not go."

"Oh, come on. Where else are we going to see a live platypus?" This was Jack's feeble attempt at a joke. His once-irrepressible wit still occasionally tossed one out, but Theo never laughed any more.

"We can see one on the Nature Channel back home."

"That's good enough for you, is it? To see something on TV? Figures."

And so it went, over the cracked and sliced bodies of the small sea creatures. As it turned out, they did take the ferry to the Taronga Park Zoo that day, and even saw a live platypus. But neither of them enjoyed it very much.

Two years ago, Jack had discovered that Theo was sleeping with a line cook at the restaurant where he worked. Theo had always maintained that he was bisexual, at least in theory, but the fact that the line cook was a woman made Jack feel doubly betrayed. It was as if Theo had rejected not just him, but his very maleness.

The affair was not serious, and Theo had already broken it off by the time Jack found out. The line cook no longer worked at Theo's restaurant, and Theo swore he didn't know or care where she had gone. They decided to stay together, not so much because they believed they had anything worth saving as because the idea of being alone after so many years frightened them both too much.

It is said that such betrayals may be forgiven, but can never be forgotten. Jack could do neither. Despite how the memory tore at him—or perhaps because of that tearing—he was never able to let it go. For longer than he cared to remember he pictured Theo with the woman and felt disgusted with his own body, could not bear to look at himself in the mirror or let Theo see him unclothed, let alone touch him. Even now, twenty-four months later, he would hurl it at Theo when Theo was least expecting it, in the most irrelevant situations possible, in the ugliest terms possible. "Oh, I'm not good enough for you because I don't have a pussy. Or tits maybe? Is that it?"

Surrender no weapon, even if it is as likely to blow up in your face as to hurt your enemy, even if you realize it is impossible for the battle ever to be won.

The afternoon light on the ocean's surface was a punishing thing, glittering coldly like diamonds, reflecting back up into their eyes. Within a couple of hours their faces were painfully sunburned. Small waves lapped against them, momentarily soothing but eventually turning their skin chapped and salty.

"The boat'll come for us," said Theo. "They'll get back to Cairns and see they forgot us. They'll shit themselves. They'll be back."

"But will we still be here?" said Jack. Theo realized it was a good question; they had no way of knowing how far they'd drifted from the site of the dive.

They had inflated their BCDs and lashed together their empty air tanks, creating an unwieldy flotation device to which they could cling. They linked hands across this device, helping to hold each other up.

"They'll come for us," Theo said again, with less conviction.

More time passed; they could not tell how much. They were very thirsty. They had stopped talking at all. The sun sank lower in the sky, and the water took on a bloody tinge.

Suddenly Jack lifted his head. "Listen," he said, and then they both heard it: the sound of rotors chopping the air. A helicopter! They could see it in the distance, a chitinous speck in the gloaming. They both began to shout. Jack let go of the air tanks and struggled in the water, trying to remove his swim trunks. When he had them off, he waved them above his head, a red flag that seemed hopelessly small in the vastness.

The helicopter passed far to their right, circled a time or two more, then headed away. They screamed at it until their throats were raw even though they knew the people inside could not possible hear them over the rotors and the wind. Theo laid his head against the air tanks and began to cry. Jack looked at him, then looked away toward where the helicopter had disappeared.

"We could try to swim back," he said.

Theo choked on a sob, tried to catch his breath. His nose was running, and he ducked his face into the water to clear it. "The hell we could. Weren't you listening to the captain? He said the reef was fifty kilometers from Cairns."

"We may have drifted closer."

"Not that much closer. Not possible. And we wouldn't even know which direction to swim."

"We'd go the way the chopper went."

"Which way was that?"

Jack looked around, started to speak, shook his head. He raised his arm out of the water to point, hesitated, then put it down.

"I don't know either," said Theo, gripping Jack's hands

more tightly. They managed to heave themselves high enough on the air tanks to lay their heads together, and each felt a tiny bit of comfort, a spark in the cold salt void.

✣

They'd taken a rental car in Sydney and begun the long drive north along the coastal highway, heading for Cairns, the jumping-off point for dive tours of the Great Barrier Reef. Their love of scuba diving was one of the first things they'd discovered they had in common, a thing they had traveled all over the world to enjoy together. They shared a sense of awe for the depths, an appreciation of the sea's majesty that neither of them had ever encountered in anyone else.

It seemed an eternity since their last diving trip off the western coast of Jamaica, but they knew the Reef was supposed to be one of the most spectacular dives on earth; it was a big part of what had brought them to Australia. Driving all the way to Cairns had been Theo's idea. He'd wanted to detour into the outback along the way, but Jack had vetoed the idea on the grounds that it would be full of choking dust, black flies, and poofter-hating rednecks.

They made good time the first day, driving almost ten hours, then found a room in a small hotel in Brisbane. They had thought to push on the following day, but in morning's light Brisbane proved to be a lovely city, dotted with fountains and sculptures and even a windmill, frosted here and there with lacy ironwork balconies that reminded them of New Orleans' French Quarter. They had last been in New Orleans nine years ago, so the memories were good. They booked their hotel room for another two nights.

The next day they climbed Mount Coot-tha, an easy two-hour hike through slender trees with sunlight slanting through their branches. At the summit, Brisbane spread before them like an exquisite miniature painting, and they could see the rocky humps of islands in the bay. They lingered on the summit and found themselves alone. Jack came up behind Theo, embraced him and whispered in his ear.

"I *do* love you. You know that, you must know that. I'm

sorry I've been so awful the past few days. I could never have come here with anyone else."

"Me either," said Theo, and squeezed Jack's long fingers tightly in his own. "Let's just forget the past few days and enjoy the rest of the trip."

They were too tired from the hike to have sex that night, or perhaps they were just afraid of risking the fragile peace they'd forged. But they talked for hours over dinner and wine, the kind of amiable, inconsequential talk they hadn't had in recent memory, and they slept curled tightly in each other's arms.

The car wouldn't start the next morning, though, and they had to wait four hours for a man from the rental agency to show up with a replacement, and they began to snarl at each other again. By the time they had transferred their luggage to the new car and were heading back up the coastal highway, a heavy silence hung between them. The greatest pain was this: each remembered the magic of the previous day on the mountain and the words they had spoken, but none of it mattered.

✢

The owner of Sea Pearl Diving Tours had been dressing down his instructor for nearly an hour, but this did not change the fact that the instructor had somehow failed to do a headcount after the last dive. Only when the boat got back to Cairns did anyone realize that two of the passengers were missing.

"Do you realize the odds of finding those people at this point?"

"Yes," the instructor said miserably.

"Do you realize that you will be directly responsible for their deaths if they aren't found?"

"Yes."

"Do you have any idea how much their families will be able to sue us for? You know how fuckin' litigious Americans are!"

The instructor did not answer this last question, as he had no idea how such things worked. He was just a diver who was barely good enough to teach people the rudiments of scuba diving, but he tried to take care of his groups. The worst thing that had ever happened on one of his dives prior to this was a German woman who had been badly stung by a box jellyfish. She'd been in a lot of pain and mad as hell, but ultimately she had been fine. He doubted the two Americans were going to be fine.

"They're being searched for?"

"Yes, you fuckin' wanker, they're *being searched for*. We've got a helicopter and three boats combing a hundred-kilometer area of the sea. A bit like finding the proverbial needle in the haystack, wouldn't you say?"

The instructor wouldn't say anything at all. He only just managed to stand up and get himself out of the owner's office before the hot tears of his shame began to flow.

+

North of Brisbane, Theo and Jack crossed into the Tropic of Capricorn. The land became brown and scorched-looking, and they had to turn on the rental car's air conditioner, which first worked abominably, then not at all. The tightening fist of the heat did nothing to improve their tempers. The scenery grew monotonous: jagged volcanic outcroppings stabbing into a dull reddish sky. Closer to Cairns there would be dripping, steaming rain forest, but here there was nothing for the eye to rest upon.

They made their next overnight stop in Mackay, the heart of the sugar cane belt that began north of Brisbane and ran all the way up the coast past Cairns. Something about the cane intrigued Jack, and he wanted to explore the town. Theo, who had driven all day, had a pounding headache. In the hotel, he pulled the curtains and went to bed while it was still light. Jack ventured out alone.

He walked through the straight streets, along the windy riverfront, past an incongruously large shopping mall and a sign notifying him that he was leaving the Mackay town limits. Then he was in the sugar cane fields. Cane towered over his head, dark purple, thick-jointed, leafy. The sky was beginning to darken. In the distance he saw a column of smoke rising over the fields, then orange flames flickering through the cane. Somebody was burning off a field before the harvest! Jack had read of this practice, which removed the leaves and was said to sweeten the cane, but he had not hoped for the extraordinary good luck of actually seeing it done, had not even known it was the right time of year.

He stood at the edge of the road watching the fire for a long time. Its fierce color and wild motion drained the sluggishness of the long car ride from him. He did not wish Theo was with him. He felt unusually free, unusually *himself*. Out here, away from his lover of a dozen years, he was only Jack. He was no longer the bickering, blaming Jack of Jack-and-Theo, though he knew he would be that Jack again tomorrow. He realized he hardly knew this Jack any more, this man standing alone on a country road on the other side of the world from his home, watching sugar cane burn.

For the thousandth or the millionth time, he thought of leaving, of walking on through the cane fields to the next town, of catching a train or a bus back to Sydney. His wallet and his passport were in his pocket. He could go.

He thought about this for a while. Then he remembered Theo's headache; the pain in Theo's eyes had been genuine and slightly desperate. He could not bear the idea of leaving Theo to fall asleep in pain and wake up alone. Perhaps that was only his latest excuse, but it was true.

Jack turned away from the bright flames and retraced his steps back through the cane fields, back into the town, back to the hotel where Theo slept.

Somehow, clinging to each other across the lashed-together air tanks, Jack and Theo dozed fitfully through the night. They were cold when they woke at dawn, but the terrible thirst had eased a little. They both knew it would return in the full light of day.

As the sun rose in the wrong direction across the sky, they saw a plane circling low above the ocean's surface, far away.

A little later they saw a boat on the horizon. They shouted and waved just as they had done before, but none of it made any difference.

"I'm tired," said Theo.

There was a crack in his voice, and at another time Jack might have latched onto that and shaken it like a pit bull. Instead he only said, "I know."

"Do you think we have any chance at all?"

Jack began to answer, but then his head jerked up and his eyes widened. He stared at Theo, mute, obviously terrified.

"What?"

"I felt something brush my leg," said Jack.

They looked down through the clear water and saw huge dark torpedo-shapes circling lazily below.

"Sharks."

"The dive instructor said they wouldn't bother people."

"Yeah, I'd put a lot of stock in what the dive instructor said."

They were quiet for a while, staring down at the dark circling shapes. The sharks made no attempt to approach them, not yet. But the psychological effect was that of a man lost in the desert who sees the first vultures overhead.

"We're going to die," said Theo. It was not a question, not even a half-veiled plea for denial or comfort; it was nothing but a statement of fact.

"Come here," said Jack, and let go of the air tanks.

They shucked their inflatable life vests and gave them to the current. Theo kicked off his fins and his swim trunks, and they pressed their bodies together, making a line of warmth in the slight chill of the ocean. The water was a great buoyant hand cradling them as they held each other. They sometimes still had sex, but it had been years since they'd really kissed. They kissed now, softly, remembering the feel and taste of each other's mouths; then harder, with teeth and tongues, with fingers tangling in each other's wet hair.

"You've got a one-track mind," said Theo, and they both laughed. It was something he had said to Jack in the early, sex-drenched days of their relationship, when they could not get enough of each other.

Their hands crept lower, beneath the water line. Their cocks were two rigid columns of flesh. They no longer felt the cold water, had no awareness of the depths yawning beneath them; it was like being in bed together years ago, knowing and feeling nothing outside their world of two-made-one.

They did not trust death to give them that fabled final orgasm. They gave it to each other with their hands and the friction of their bodies, and their seed mingled with the ocean, the salty essence of their lives returning to its primordial home, a triumph over the void as well as an acceptance of it.

Then they held each other very tightly and let the tanks float away. They did not want to be taken, to wonder who would go first, to see each other ripped apart, the pool of blood spreading like an oil slick on the water's surface. Instead, they took one last breath in unison, savoring the seldom-noticed sweetness of air, and dived together forever.

THE OCEAN

It was right after the fight with Niccolo that Eli went for his last drive.

The fight wouldn't have been such a big deal under normal circumstances, if there was such a thing as "normal circumstances" for the members of Fly any more. There had been fights before, and plenty of them. But this particular one touched on a lot of things that had preyed on Eli's mind lately. Such as the champagne and the feather pillows.

Eli had come back to his hotel room late one night after a concert, dead tired and lathered with dry sweat, sure he'd be asleep before he hit the mattress. He'd found Niccolo in his room with a very young Asian girl. They each had a bottle of champagne and were trying to pour it into each other's mouths. Most of it was going all over them and the bed. Eli's bed. Niccolo's trousers were drenched with it. The girl's breasts were slick with foam. The room reeked of champagne, sharp and sour. The floor was covered with a creamy pale fluff. Eli couldn't figure that out until he saw the flaccid pillowcases in a heap at the foot of the bed.

"We had a pillow fight," said Niccolo.

"Looks like a blizzard hit, hey?" said the Asian girl, and giggled.

Eli went to sleep in Niccolo's room. He woke at seven the next morning with a silvery-delicate headache and a sense of heaviness and warmth and rancid champagne on the bed beside him. The Asian girl had gone into a leaden doze on Eli's bed, and Niccolo couldn't stand to sleep on the wet mattress next to her. His tangled brown hair was spread out on the pillow next to Eli's face, and his legs were sprawled out under the covers, flung across Eli's. Eli kicked them away.

Then there was the blurb in the fan magazine. It was one of those magazines that had words like PIX and INFO and SIZZLING COLOR plastered all over its cover, and fold-out posters of himself or Niccolo, or sometimes Bailey or Jock, or any combination of the four. The magazine was in Niccolo's suitcase; people gave those magazines to the guitarist, and he saved them to pore over obsessively when he was alone. There was a tall stack of them in his bedroom at home that he kept saying he was going to throw out, but Niccolo hadn't been home for months: the other three had taken a week off in the middle of their world tour and gone home, but Niccolo had gone to Paris to shop for rare occult books. The fans, who had nicknames for all of them, called Niccolo the Spook.

Eli picked up the magazine and flipped through it. He knew it would put him in a bad mood for the rest of the day, and was about to toss it back onto Niccolo's bed when he saw a picture of himself and Marie. The caption said:

> Elijah Stiles of Fly, resplendent in black velvet trousers and leopard-skin jacket (fake—eccentric Eli labels himself a hardcore animal lover and is even considering becoming a vegetarian!!!). But that gorgeous mane of blonde hair is always real! He attended this Broadway opening with an unidentified beauty.

"Unidentified beauty." That was his girlfriend of two and a half years, and the magazine writers knew it, and Eli knew they knew it. But the fans didn't know it, and didn't want to. It might disturb them. The fans, all the little girls, had to be sheltered from gossip column scandals and innuendo. They might get upset, tear the pinups off their bedroom walls, stop buying the records. No, you couldn't break the little girls' hearts. Marie had to stay reduced to a nonentity, an unidentified beauty.

And there were the natty clothes, velvet frock coats, flowered silk shirts, trousers made of fabric that looked like striped Christmas candy. He got so sick of beautiful clothes that he went around naked at home. There was the way his hair felt stiff and dry at the ends because he hadn't cut it in two years; the fans liked it long. There was Niccolo's lovely young-old face. Early in the tour, Niccolo had fallen into a drunken sleep at an all-night party. When people began pouring half-empty glasses of beer over his head, Eli decided it was time to get him out of the way. Niccolo was so slight and thin that Eli was able to pick him up like a child and carry him back to his room. As he was draping a blanket over Niccolo, he looked at the small familiar face, the smooth cheeks, the impossibly straight nose. And he realized with something like dread that there were tiny lines around Niccolo's eyes. Niccolo often wore dark eyeliner for performances. That night's layer was still smeared around his eyes. It had crept capillary-like into the creases of his eyelids, forming a spiderweb pattern around his eyes. The breath from between his parted lips was sweet and spicy with wine. One hand was flung up on the pillow next to his face, loosely curled, with a delicate golden chain looped twice around its wrist. In the sleep of alcohol Niccolo was childlike, but the lines around his eyes made Eli see him ten years from now, wrung dry, his life the equivalent of a few faded rose petals on the floor of a ballroom. Then Eli became afraid that he would lose his own looks, and hated himself for caring. But Niccolo was twenty-five, and that was too young to have lines around your eyes.

Yes, it would have been a rough life if they weren't all hugely successful at their chosen career and filthy rich to boot.

That was one of the things Niccolo told Eli during the fight. "Right," Niccolo said with that annoying quirk of his Cupid lips that Eli had become so used to. "Right. I bet there are lots of workers in South Africa who would just *love* to hear you pull the covers over your head and moan about how tough it is to be Elijah Stiles. They'd really feel for you, my friend."

"That isn't the point. No, I'm not going to give it up. I'm not going to go live on a kibbutz and raise fucking soybeans. But that doesn't mean I want the leopard either."

They were arguing about a public appearance Fly was scheduled to make at a record store in Virginia. Their publicist had hired and animal trainer to bring a full-grown leopard to the gig, a play on the fact that the big single from their album was called "Danger Spots." Usually Eli endured the hype, comforting himself with the notion that anything went as long as they didn't prostitute their actual music. Usually he wore the costume of golden rock god without complaint, cut whatever ribbons needed cutting, obligingly turned the bottle toward the photographers and let the champagne foam into Niccolo's glass.

The leopard caused him to rebel. In the first place, he told the publicist, the song's lyrics were about symbolic spots, not the real things on a leopard's hide. In the second place, the animal would obviously have to be drugged to the eyeballs and didn't need to spend the afternoon in a hot mall full of screaming teenage girls who would inevitably want to pat its head. It was the sickest form of conspicuous consumption, he told everyone, the degradation of a living thing. Finally Eli said he would only attend the appearance if the leopard did not, and the contract of the trainer and beast was canceled. In the world of rock music, a band without its singer was a handicapped band. The trainer had to make up for the lost gig, and someone later told Eli that the big cat had ended up appearing that afternoon at the grand opening of a supermarket.

Eli spent most of the day in bed, at peace in the shady room until Niccolo stormed in, flicked on the overhead light, and accused him of trying to take over the band. They railed at each other for what seemed like several hours, until the others were lured in by the sound of their raised voices. Jock lounged on the bed next to Eli, interested. Bailey faded uncomfortably into the bathroom. Soon tiny plops and hisses were audible; Bailey liked to toss aspirin tablets into the toilet and watch them explode. Eli and Niccolo paused for breath and went on arguing. Jock jumped up and slipped out the door, heading down the hall toward Niccolo's room. In a moment he returned with one of Niccolo's guitars. He perched his considerable bulk on the floor and began to strum. Jock was widely acknowledged as the hardest-hitting drummer on the scene, but he played guitar very badly and sang worse. "ALL WE ARE SAAAAY—ING," he wailed, "IS GIVE PEACE A CHAAAAAANCE."

He was so ridiculous that they had to laugh, which dissipated most of the tension in the room. Eli threw the bedclothes back and crossed the room to put his arm around Niccolo. Niccolo's shoulders were stiff, and when he wasn't smiling, his lips still had that hateful quirk. Eli knew there would be plenty of juicy arguments before the matter of the leopard and all the overtones Niccolo supposed it had were settled.

Eli wasn't up for it today. He cleared everyone out of his room under the pretense of taking a nap. Then he rose and dressed (a plain white T-shirt and old faded jeans with a red bandanna patch at one knee, and God, didn't they feel better than velvet jackets and pants so tight his balls couldn't breathe) and left the room.

There was a crowd of teenagers outside, completely surrounding the hotel. They were holding a vigil, boosted every few hours by a glimpse of Eli, Niccolo, Bailey, or Jock. At the concierge desk Eli arranged to rent a car for the afternoon. Driving had always relaxed him, especially if he could drive fast. They were in California, and the concierge informed him there was a Jaguar XKE coupe with a 4.2-litre engine available. He could take it out to the desert and let it rip.

As Eli turned to leave, the concierge looked worried. "Are you sure you don't want me to find someone to accompany you to the car, Mr. Stiles? Kids get excited and don't always know what they're doing..."

"They're my fans. I can handle them." He refrained from pointing out how many times and in how many ways he *had* handled them, and simply asked the man to have the car brought around for him.

The girls were upon Eli as soon as he stepped outside. He was overwhelmed with the scents of perfume and watermelon bubble gum. Rose petals wafted around him and settled in his hair. A bunch of grapes was shoved into his hands, a reference to a Roman bacchanal in his lyrics. Brave little fingers touched him as lightly as wings. He smiled tolerantly. All of them had been through this too many times to count. He pressed gently through the crowd, afraid they'd hurt themselves if he moved too quickly. He was almost to the car when the pain stabbed through his wrist.

"*Jesus*!" For a few seconds he felt as if a white-hot needle had been pushed into his vein. He whirled on the crowd and studied their faces. Brushing him with their fingertips was one thing, but he was damned if he was going to let them hurt him. Their faces were all alike, innocuously pretty, heavily made up, very young. An occasional hand poked out of the crowd, grabbing at him. He dropped the bunch of grapes. They pounced on it immediately. He heard the fruit squelching as they fought over it.

Only when the car's door handle poked him in the small of his back did Eli realize he had been backing away from the crowd. He gave a feeble little wave, which elevated the girls to new heights of gasping and pointing, and fumbled with the key. A sense of relief seeped through him when he was inside the locked car.

Eli examined his wounded wrist. No wonder the girls had pointed at it when he waved—a fat worm of blood was running down his inner forearm. Tiny threads of scarlet crept through the fine blonde hairs there, reminding him of the fine lines around Niccolo's eyes...which had most likely been simple exhaustion. And the scratch on his wrist, which was already clotting up, hadn't been maliciously inflicted upon him by a groupie with blood lust. Probably one of the girls had been wearing a pin that had come undone, or had had something sharp sticking out of her handbag. Marie once had to have three stitches after gashing her finger on a razor blade buried deep in her purse. She used razors to cut her canvases and scrape paint off her wooden palette, but this one had hidden and turned on her. Eli had made her dump her purse out and throw away all the superfluous junk. Even now he smiled at the memory of some of the crap she'd had in there. Ads torn from magazines because she liked the colors, felt-tip pins and minuscule sketchpads, a red rubber dagger. She swore she'd never seen the last item before. Like Niccolo, women were natural packrats. Eli himself always ended up throwing things out and needing them later.

Girls fell across the hood of the Jag as he pulled out of the parking lot. He beeped the horn gently and inched away, one sneaker-clad food poised over the brake pedal in case any of them should jump out in front of him. They flung grapes and roses after the car. He raised a hand—the uninjured one—in thanks.

Eli drove and drove, passing glossy storefronts, box-format office buildings, hotels like their own, but not as comfortable or well-located. He drove past a bus station and thought how well he liked flying. Niccolo hated it. His slender, skilled fingers would dig into the leather of his armrest as the plane took off, and though he liked watching the heaven-like formations of clouds and sunlight outside the window, he refused to look down if the crisscross patterns of roads and buildings on the ground were visible. Flying over bodies of water was out of the question unless Niccolo had had at least three drinks in the airport lounge.

The car drifted toward the center of the road. Eli righted it. He had left the middle of the city and was driving on the outskirts, past dingy convenience marts, Bowlaramas, nightclubs shut darkly against the daylight. Soon the only buildings were gas stations and fruit stands scattered along the highway. The air was clear, but there was a faint reddish haze in the distance where the mountains met the sky. Niccolo and the leopard and Jock's funny-desperate attempt at peacemaking began to fade. He rolled his window down and drove out into the desert. The powerful engine purred beneath him, responsive as a groupie's body. The sun seemed to sear away all his earthly concerns. The landscape was cleansing: so empty, his eyes might have been filled with sand.

It was dark when he got back to the hotel. The others weren't around; no doubt their manager had dragged them off to some club and they would all be wondering loudly where he was. Eli took a long shower, fell into bed, and dreamed of empty, shifting sands. His sleep wasn't long enough. It never was.

✦

"Time to be Elijah Stiles," said Niccolo.

They were backstage at a massive arena, could have been anywhere in the States. Eli had just shared a massive line of coke with Jock, and the walls of the dressing room seemed to swarm with motes of sand. Niccolo examined himself in the mirror. His hair was a wild dark cloud, his eyes sunken shadows in his face. Eli closed his eyes and shivered. He was wearing a white silk suit embroidered with astrological symbols; it was indeed time to be Elijah Stiles, to play the role. But most of all it was time to sing. No amount of hype and false glory could dull that feeling.

And it was glorious. He was in full voice and the music poured from Niccolo's fingers with the smoothness of sex. The band was utterly together. Bailey and Jock laid down a solid base of rhythm. Niccolo peeked from under his eyelashes and filled the stage with strange chords, pyramids of a thousand notes. Midway through the show, Eli leaned his body against Niccolo's as their respective instruments howled together, and things were all right between them again.

And the boys banged their heads, and the little girls cried and reached and screamed.

✦

Eli woke the next morning with a fresh sense of purpose. He felt good. He had partied after the show, but only for a few hours; he'd had little to drink, less to snort, and hadn't touched the smack at all. Best of all, he had woken up alone. Marie's beautiful face would not hover accusingly before him today.

He showered and washed his hair. The scratch on his wrist pulsed. He felt drawn to the desert again.

Today's concierge—a woman this time—smiled up at him. "Same car as yesterday, Mr. Stiles?"

"Yes please, ma'am," he said, making her his for life. "Can you have it brought round?"

The car wasn't there yet when he stepped out of the lobby. The girls still circled the hotel. Love was in their eyes as they surged forward to greet him. Their hands reached; some of them were almost touching him now. Their fingers were tipped with sharp slivers of red, and their mouths were wet, and their sound was one communal babble that rose in pitch and volume as they approached him.

A soft little hand closed on Eli's wrist. The wounded one. There was a flash of pain. He felt the lips of the cut part, the blood begin to flow again. The girl's head bowed over his hand. Her hair was an impossibly pale shade of blonde, but natural right down to the roots; it would darken before she turned sixteen. Other pneumatic young bodies pressed against him. Their softness surrounded him. He cursed himself for not having his manager beside him, or the concierge, or *someone*.

The girls. The red slivers at their fingertips. Their wet mouths.

Eli looked at his wrist, at the girl's mouth on it. The flesh had separated from the bone in a curious way, in two neat flaps. There was only a thin lather of blood, but the pain was deeper, more personal, more surely *his* than he had ever imagined pain could be. It went beyond pain, beyond emotion. He was only looking on. He closed his eyes and felt delicate tendrils of agony, as fine as the lines around Niccolo's eyes, wrap around him and lift him away.

The little girls snapped at anyone who tried to come near. The police were summoned, but even when it became obvious what the girls were doing, no policeman would club them or shoot at them. There were so many, and they were so pretty, and none of them was over sixteen.

At last they had to be allowed to feed until they were sated.

For Neil Gaiman, with gratitude

MARISOL

You could say it was a bad patch in my life. I'd been suspended from my position as coroner of New Orleans following allegations of negligence in the Devlin Lemon case (these were ultimately resolved and I am now back at work). My dalliance with rock god Kyle Gass of Tenacious D was testing the patience of my long-suffering husband, Seymour. (Most D groupies prefer Jack Black, but I've always had a bit of a fetish for sidekicks.) I suppose it was only natural that I would fall in with the crowd at Marisol. They were a hard-drinking bunch, but they kept me well fed.

Marisol is a bit of a fluke on the New Orleans restaurant scene. Chef Peter Vazquez failed to endear himself to the old-line dining crowd when he told the *Times-Picayune* restaurant critic, "You'll never see crawfish or maque choux on my menu." I have heard that in the wake of this (excellent) review, Chef Pete was anonymously sent a pound of crawfish, each one dressed in a tiny ghost costume. The gift card read,

"YOUR WORDS WILL HAUNT YOU FOREVER." That right there should tell you a great deal about the psychotic, meunière-drenched ways of New Orleans' old-line dining crowd. Most of them are happy to sit quietly dipping the splintery legs of their fried softshell crabs into the pools of brown butter on their plates, but a few feel compelled to police the eating habits of everyone else in the city. Perhaps you've heard of the Food Police, those guardians of cardiovascular health who seem to take sadistic pleasure in announcing that your favorite foods are bad for you. In New Orleans the Food Police don't care about your health, but they exercise constant vigilance against vegetarians, exotic ethnic cuisines, and any dish that hasn't been on the city's menus since 1870 or so. You should see their arteries when they die—cross-section one and it looks exactly like a Krispy Kreme doughnut.

At any rate, Marisol has been on the radar of the New Orleans Food Police since 1999. The place is infamous for "weird" flavor combinations, "disgusting" use of organ meats and offal, and a cheese list whose very excess seems to offend a city known for its excesses. (There were over forty cheeses on the list at last count, each served with its own housemade garnish.) Consider the Maine lobster wrapped in a crispy pig's ear with baby bok choy, toasted rice cake, and XO sauce. This was, quite simply, one of the best dishes I've eaten anywhere in my life. The lobster was the tenderest I've ever had, and it soaked up the combined flavors of the pork fat, the sweet glaze, and the spicy XO sauce to form a heavenly gestalt. The pig's ear had been simmered for days so that it was also fork-tender, but retained some of its interesting gelatinous crunch. A pass through a blowtorch flame had caramelized the surface of the dish, making it dark and crackly. I ate every bite, then licked the plate, then gnawed on the rim. Since Pete has a repertoire of about eight hundred dishes and seldom repeats himself, I feel lucky to have had this dish the way you might feel lucky to have glimpsed Garbo on a Paris street or seen Charlie Parker play at Birdland. But it's the sort of thing that can inflame New Orleans as surely as claiming KFC makes better chicken than Popeye's.

(Popeye's Fried Chicken, incidentally, was founded in New Orleans. Possibly you know that, but it seems we seldom receive credit for our principal products simply because no one believes we're capable of producing anything beyond voodoo, jazz, and alligator-foot backscratchers. I once played tour guide to a pair of Bay Area pathologists who must have been jaded from the experience of living in a real city. As we drove past Ruth's Chris Steak House on Broad Street, I commented, "That's the original Ruth's Chris," and they said, "Oh, we thought it started in San Francisco, because we have them there." A while later we drove past the Calliope housing project. I said, "There's where Dirty King grew up," and they replied, "Oh, we thought he was from Oakland, because we saw one of his billboards in our neighborhood." No acknowledgement whatsoever that we might birth our own steak chains and rap stars. This sort of cultural *droit de seigneur*, if you will, boils my blood so thoroughly that I can't bear to discuss it any further.)

On the shady section of Esplanade Avenue that separates the French Quarter and the Faubourg Marigny, in a pretty whitewashed brick building with a blue-and-white-striped awning, Marisol appears to be a charming little restaurant. There are sunflowers painted on the walls of the dining room and a lush sun-dappled courtyard in the back. For casual diners I imagine it is a charming little restaurant, nothing more. For serious food people it is a Mecca with more than a little of that city's underlying mystery and danger. These days, "Mecca" is used indiscriminately to describe any place people wish to visit, but one would do well to recall that infidels have been murdered for sneaking into Mecca. This is the kind of thing that doesn't seem out of the realm of possibility at Marisol. The stakes there are high enough to guarantee a spectacular dining experience, but too high for real comfort. If you are paying close attention, there's an edge to everything at Marisol.

To wit: The pumpkin-carving contest. I was the celebrity guest. You may well ponder the wisdom of promoting your business via a disgraced coroner cutting a face in a nogginlike gourd. Everyone at Marisol thought it was a great idea, so on the Saturday before Halloween, I arrived at the restaurant with a handful of not-so-sharp scalpels. Tenacious D had arrived in town that afternoon to play a show at the House of Blues, and I was aching to see Kyle, but I'd promised to do this event first. Janis Vazquez greeted me at the door. Married to Chef Pete for four years, she is co-owner of the restaurant and acts as hostess, manager, accountant, P.R. flak, and raconteur. Despite the occasional outbursts of utter despair that come with the territory of owning a restaurant, she always looks cool and exotically pretty, and I was glad to see her. "Kyle's in town," I said. "What should I do?"

"Well, let's see. I know—you should go to his hotel room and refuse to leave until the two of you have spent at least three hours fucking like bunnies."

"But what about Seymour?"

"Ahhh, hell. Give him a hundred one-dollar bills and tell him to spend the evening at the Hustler Club."

"That's sick, Janis."

"You cut off the tops of people's skulls with an electric saw, and you call me sick," said Janis. "I adore your logic, Dr. Brite. And speaking of cutting off the tops of skulls, we've got the pumpkins all ready out back."

Janis fixed me a glass of Wild Turkey and ice with a splash of soda, and I walked through the restaurant to the courtyard. Several of the waiters, waitresses, and regular customers were selecting pumpkins from a pile by the fountain. Chef Pete and Shayne the bartender sat slumped at a table in a shady corner of the courtyard. I gripped my drink in one hand, hoisted a large, warty pumpkin under the other arm, and walked over to them. They lifted their heads at the sound of my approach, but then their chins sank toward their chests again as if the effort had been too much. Though they were both big, strapping men, today they appeared somehow diminished. Pete's slate-blue eyes were red-rimmed and crusty, and pain dulled their usual manic gleam. Shayne's fair Irish complexion had gone hectically blotchy. "What in the world have you two been *doing*?" I said.

"You have to ask?" said Pete, and laughed his depraved-sounding laugh.

"Well, drinking, I assume. But I've seen you hung over before, and you didn't look like this."

"It was a really extreme night," said Shayne. "At least I think it was."

There followed a litany of half-recollections, that odd combination of boast and remorse unique to the badly hungover: "I found my keys in the trash this morning." "I found my *head* in the trash this morning." "Do you remember putting all the cocktail shakers in my car?" "Do you remember spitting on that hippie?" "When I got home, even my dog wouldn't come near me." "Dude, I didn't even *get* home."

I waited for them to wind down. When they fell silent, I said, "Was there some special reason for this bacchanal, or did you just decide you hadn't suffered enough lately?"

"Oh, I've suffered," said Pete. "I've suffered, all right. Look."

From under the table he pulled a copy of *Big Easy*, a glossy magazine left as a freebie in many of the city's upscale hotel rooms and lobbies. It fell open to a dog-eared page. I took the magazine and began to read a review of Marisol by *Big Easy*'s restaurant critic, Lianne Apple. It wasn't so much a bad review as a completely clueless one.

> …it seems to me that Vazquez is making snazzy fusion food that doesn't disappoint, but frequently confuses. Why complicate a perfectly decent duck confit by putting it in an Asian-tasting broth? Why wrap a nice piece of lobster in a pig's ear? Where are the connections? Is he simply trying to be weird? I liked much of what I ate at Marisol, but I never quite felt that I "got" it.

I frowned, not quite getting it myself. Pete had received stupid reviews before, and even the good reviews of Marisol usually contained a stupid comment or two. He was operating at a level too eclectic for many critics, who must search out common denominators of taste.

But as I scanned the rest of the page, I saw what had

unhinged him. At the end of the review was a section called "Tidbits" where Apple listed restaurant news and miscellania. Here she had written, "Kudos to Escargot's at the Hotel Bienvenu for its spectacularly overhauled cheese cart! Now offering fourteen different selections including Valdeon, Laura Chenel goat cheese, and Manchego, this list is a peerless journey through *le monde du fromage*."

I'd ordered from the cheese cart at Escargot's, and the waiter had appalled me by slicing all my cheeses with the same knife so that their flavors contaminated one another. I skimmed the Marisol review again. Apple hadn't even mentioned Pete's forty-plus cheeses, only commenting that his dessert menu seemed "surprisingly light," whatever that meant. Pete was obsessive about everything to do with his menu, but the cheese list was his special baby. Ignoring it while giving props to a lesser list on the same page was tantamount to a declaration of war.

"'Is he simply trying to be weird?'" quoted Shayne, and they both cackled like demons, then clutched their heads. Pete waved one of the waitresses over and said, "Would you get me the Tylenol, Nora?"

"A Tylenol?"

"No, *the* Tylenol. The whole *bottle*."

"That's not good for your liver after alcohol," I said automatically.

"You know what, Doc?" said Pete.

"You don't give a fuck?"

"Right."

I picked up my scalpel and began to carve my jack o'lantern, but it was difficult to concentrate on forming perfect evil eyes and needle-sharp teeth. I worried about Janis and Pete, and about Marisol. Restaurants are very important to me, and I am committed to making sure my favorites thrive—that was why I was on an unpaid vacation just now. I had no doubts about the quality of the restaurant, but as I have said, Pete set the stakes almost impossibly high. I feared he would eventually self-destruct. Hell, I feared I might be self-destructing, and I wanted to be certain of eating well until I did so.

Tenacious D and their entourage had arranged to stay over a few days in New Orleans, and I brought them to a wine dinner at Marisol. Seymour came too—he is a very patient man, though trying at times. I sat at the head of the table with him on one side and Kyle on the other, and I felt giddy with happiness. I would drink all the wine pairings, I decided, though I had already had two Wild Turkey and sodas. I could do it. I was invincible.

The last thing I really remember is asking Jack Black whether Gwyneth Paltrow was really as vapid as she looked. "Or is her face just made that way?" I think I said. I don't remember his reply, or any of the subsequent events except in awful, jumpy flashes like something Oliver Stone might have left on the cutting-room floor. There's Pete behind the bar pouring himself a shot of tequila; I stick out my empty glass; "You don't really want one," he says; "Yes I do," I leer. There's me staggering to the patio doors, only to find them locked; somehow it's suddenly very late. There's me bending at the waist and puking on the nice hardwood bar floor, thinking I am being very discreet. There's Seymour pouring me into our car while Kyle stands on the curb shouting, "Go for it, buddy." There's me calling the flower shop the next day, whispering through my hangover, ordering a dozen white and a dozen red roses sent to Marisol with a note that says "Sorry about your floor."

Janis called two days after the wine dinner to thank me for the flowers and tell me the restaurant would be closed a week for kitchen repairs. "How was Kyle's visit?" she asked.

"He hasn't called me since the wine dinner. I think watching me vomit a seven-course meal may have taken the romance out of it for him."

"His loss," Janis said kindly.

"Yeah, I guess. How's Pete?"

"Oh, you know. Still bitching about that damn *Big Easy* review. If I were Lianne Apple, I wouldn't feel safe in my own home."

I laughed at that, because I thought she was kidding.

Even when the *Times-Picayune* reported that Lianne Apple was missing, I didn't think much of it. The newspaper story said she had been estranged from her husband for several months and that he was a primary suspect in her kidnapping. Foul play seemed almost certain. Readers learned any number of sordid details about Apple, including the fact that she had been born with a congenital defect in her heart. Surgeons had cracked her chest and patched it up years ago, but she still had a fragile ticker. An anonymous police spokesperson opined that even if an assailant hadn't meant to really hurt her, a good shock could have literally scared her to death.

The husband, located and interrogated, declared his innocence in increasingly desperate tones. To no avail: he was still cooling his heels in Orleans Parish Prison when Marisol reopened. Pete sent me an e-mail titled "Come In Soon For The Most Kick-Ass Menu Ever."

I did, and it was. I ordered the Arctic char with weinkraut and received the best piece of fish I'd ever tasted. A strip of skin left on one side of the filet provided the perfect crisp contrast to the meltingly tender, unctuous pink flesh. As I was running my index finger across the plate to get the last traces of fat and kraut juice, Jason the waiter appeared at my table with another plate. "Chef wanted you to try this," he said. "He's putting it on the menu tomorrow. It's called The Offal Truth."

I think I frowned a little; Pete didn't usually go for cutesy dish names. But then Jason set the plate before me and my frown faded as I caught a whiff of it. There were thin slices of heart braised with chanterelles and coarse mustard; tripe cooked *à la niçoise* with tomatoes, garlic, and black olives; crisp sweetbreads with artichokes and caramelized onions. I dug into this bountiful organ sampler and had taken several bites before I noticed something curious. I forked up a slice of heart and examined it closely, noting the trace of old scar tissue and the distinctive marks of tiny, well-healed stitches.

I looked up and saw Pete standing by the kitchen door, the

very antithesis of the swanning, preening head chef in his unmonogrammed white jacket and scruffy check pants cut off at the knees. He grinned at me. I smiled back, put the slice of heart in my mouth, and chewed. That was when I realized I'd do just about anything to keep eating his food.

"How's the offal?" he said, coming over to the table.

"Great," I told him. "Delicious. Maybe your best idea ever. But don't serve the brain."

"Why? You worried about Creutzfield-Jacob Syndrome?"

"No," I said around a mouthful of garlicky tripe. "I'm just afraid stupidity might be contagious."

POIVRE

I'd been hearing for years about the pork blood sausage known as *boudin noir*, but I never tasted a really good version until the spring of 2001, when I began eating at a beautiful little restaurant that had just opened in my neighborhood. I'll call it Poivre (my reasons for not giving its real name will become apparent presently).

I had thought this pretty little space would be doomed forever by the Bad Restaurant Curse: first it was a ridiculously overpriced noodle house operated by a high-toned Uptown bitch of the first order; then an earnest but not very good Spanish place; then Poivre, with a menu of impeccable French country food concocted by a chef/owner just twenty-nine years old and handsome enough to be a movie star, male model, or kept man. Whether because of the chef's outer charms or because of his talent for bringing out the sensual soul of an ingredient, my meals at Poivre were conducted in a sort of swoon. The rose-red walls, the tiny flowers on the tables, the little oil lamps turning the window glass golden at twilight, the lush appetizer of veal marrow melting into chanterelles, the huge, succulent, sluttish cherries in the pie...ah! it was an erotic dream of a restaurant. Sometimes, overcome by it all, I could only rest my head upon the gleaming surface of my favorite table and murmur, "I love this place."

Everyone else loved it too. The chef received a rave review from the daily paper, mentions in the national food press, and a glamorous cover shot for a tony local magazine (not that his cooking didn't deserve it, but every time I saw the thing on the newsstand, I had to wonder whether it would have happened if he had looked like, say, Tom Bosley). The tiny restaurant—it seated just thirty-eight—became perpetually full and loud and chaotic. Though dining there was no longer quite such a pleasant experience, we tried to feel happy for the chef. After all, we'd been there nearly from the beginning, and we still received our habitual *amuses-bouche* and other little perks of the particularly appreciated customer.

Then, one very busy night, we didn't—but the people at the next table did.

It was only a fresh fig wrapped in a piece of prosciutto, and I never even thought his prosciutto was all that good. You wouldn't dream that the absence of a single fig could pierce your heart so deeply. But we sat at our fourth-favorite table (the first through third favorites were occupied by larger parties) and watched those *other* people eating *their* figs, and the joy of an evening at Poivre slowly turned to gall and wormwood. I tried to hide my sorrow, but the maitre d' knew me well and asked what was wrong. "Oh, nothing; we didn't get an *amuse*," I said, trying to make it sound like a joke but still feeling like the most tiresome, spoiled person in the world. "Oh, the chef's in a *mood* tonight," the maitre d' told me, but I only wondered why his mood did not extend to the people at the next table.

We didn't stop going to Poivre after that. It would be silly to stop going to a beloved restaurant just because you were not given a complimentary fig. We went once more, actually in the company of the maitre d', who had never dined there and (flatteringly) wished to do so in our company on his night off. The marrow melted silkily in my mouth again, the oil lamps glowed mellow gold, the chef visited our table with a bottle of otherwise unattainable olive oil to drizzle over our *amuses-bouche*. I thought the magic of Poivre was recaptured until the waiter—not one of the young men we knew so well, but a slightly older one we hadn't seen before—cleared our salad plates. The maitre d' had left a few pieces of watercress, and the waiter put his thumb on a fork handle in such a way as to flip one of these pieces high into the air. It hung there for one dreadful second, then descended, smacking me in the face and sliding greasily down into my cleavage. The waiter turned away from our table, and worse than the sensation of vinaigrette-covered watercress in my bra was the realization that not only had an employee of Poivre been careless enough to do such a thing—he hadn't even noticed.

After the first few seconds, I was able to laugh, but I knew at that moment that I would never come here again. I wasn't precisely offended; after all, I really doubted that the waiter had *meant* to throw watercress at me. But now I knew that there was no real magic to this restaurant; like the rest of the world, it was a place where cold, greasy reality could smack you in the face without warning.

My current favorite restaurant couldn't be more different than Poivre: its walls are sunflower-yellow; its menu is an uncontrolled, sprawling, eclectically brilliant thing; its chef is a misanthropic thug with a wild talent, and no one's pretty boy—I once watched him stand behind the bar in a white undershirt, tattoos hanging out, a bottle of tequila in each hand, snarling, "What's the matter? I'm not *camera-ready*?"

They sometimes have the same *boudin noir* as Poivre, though. Turns out it comes from the distributor in a little can. Even so, it does have a lovely, rich, bloody taste.

PANSU

Twilight was settling over L.A.'s Koreatown, the lights of the stores clicking off, the lights of the restaurants and bars flickering on. Samuel Oh stood beneath the red marquee of his restaurant, surveyed the street scene, and thought that this was one of those rare California moments of peace with no evil.

He was wrong.

He went back inside. The dinner crowd had just started to come in. The restaurant was dark, lit with paper lanterns and strings of Christmas lights. Two of his favorite customers, a pair of young men who wrote and produced a successful TV show, were at their usual table in the corner. Mr. Oh's wife, Bobbi, was setting out their *pan chan*. Smiling, she laid the last of the small dishes on the table. Mr. Oh was about to turn away when he saw Bobbi hurl her tray like a Frisbee across the room, where it landed in the middle of someone's flaming bulgogi platter. She thrust her tongue out as far as it would go, hiked her modest skirt well above her waist, and commanded the two young men, "Fuck me!"

"Uh, we don't really feel that way about you, Mrs. Oh," said one of them.

"And those people's table is on fire," pointed out the other one.

Mr. Oh grabbed the fire extinguisher from its place beside the kitchen door, ran to the table where the tray had landed, and doused the flames with chemical foam, apologizing furiously to the diners. Luckily they were Korean, and he was able to express his profound embarrassment and promise them a complimentary replacement dinner without stumbling over his words. He found a waitress to move them to a new table and raced over to where his wife had begun to slide out of her white cotton panties. He grabbed her from behind. She lashed out with one arm and sent him flying backward. His feet tangled, and he fell ungracefully to the floor.

"Is your wife OK?" asked one of the young men, bending to assist Mr. Oh.

"Dude, obviously she's not OK," his friend said. As they helped Mr. Oh to his feet, Bobbi yanked the tablecloth off the table and sent the little appetizer dishes flying. A particularly spicy clump of *kimchi* hit Mr. Oh square in the left eye. Diners were beginning to flee the restaurant as Bobbi ran to the center of the room, screamed "FUCK ME, ANYBODY FUCK ME!", and vomited a mass of bright green goo into a charming little fountain Mr. Oh had just installed.

He turned desperately to the two TV writers. "What can be wrong with her?" he asked in English.

"Well," said the light-haired one, "I've only ever seen a movie about it, but it looks to me like she's possessed by Satan."

"Yup," his friend concurred. "Exorcist, obviously."

"What do you mean?" Mr. Oh began to ask, but then his wife's head spun twice around on her neck, and as he heard the terrible sound of the cracking bones he knew, because he had seen the movie himself.

Mr. Oh had closed the restaurant, sent the staff home, and dragged Bobbi into the little office where he placed the food orders and added the receipts. He had begged his two TV-writing customers to stay, as they seemed to know more than he did about this problem, and they had reluctantly agreed. In his distraction he kept mixing up their names, but he was fairly sure that the light-haired one was called Darin and the other one was Mark.

Since he usually kept the restaurant open all night, he had a little cot in the office. Bobbi thrashed on it now, her wrists bound with napkins because she had scratched her face so badly that blood and shreds of skin were embedded beneath her nails. She had torn all the buttons off her blouse before he managed to tie her up, and the sight of her plain white cotton bra against her flushed golden skin broke Mr. Oh's heart a little more. Her skirt was rucked up beneath her, her legs akimbo, her body twisting in some pain or fury he could not imagine.

He turned away from her and saw that Mark was rolling a joint on the desk where he did the accounts. The loose marijuana was scattered across a seafood bill stamped PAID, like some terrible symbol of chaos consuming order. "You cannot smoke that shit in here!"

Mark looked up at him with eyes very dark and serious. "Mr. Oh," he said, "if you want us to stay here and try to help you deal with your possessed wife, then we most definitely *can* smoke this shit in here."

Darin nodded his agreement and pulled out a Zippo lighter stamped with some vulgar cartoon character. Mark put the finished joint in his mouth and leaned over so that Darin could light it for him. They went through a complex, difficult-looking process of getting it to stay lit and burn evenly. Mr. Oh found that he could not take his eyes off this process: if he looked at them, he did not have to look at his wife writhing on the cot.

He could still hear her, though. She was muttering in Korean, dreadful words he had not thought she knew and had never imagined that she would combine. Literally, she had just called him, or someone unseen, a fucker of pigs.

The marijuana smoke filled the small office and made Mr. Oh's head feel as if it sat more lightly on his neck. For the first time since Bobbi had thrown the tray, he relaxed a little, and realized that perhaps he did know something about this problem after all.

As if sensing possible danger, Bobbi spoke up. Her words were English now, her voice so guttural it hurt to hear, with an accent that was definitely not Korean. "YOU'RE GETTING STONED!"

"No I'm not," he said without thinking.

"Dude!" Darin grabbed his arm. "*Don't answer its charges.* That's one of the rules you have to follow. It lies."

"Not necessarily in this case," Mark said. "He might *be* getting stoned. It's pretty smoky in here."

"Well, but you're not supposed to argue with it. Max von Sydow said so."

"Agreed."

"FUCKING ADDICT WASTECASE FAGGOTS!" Bobbi roared.

They glanced over at the cot, looked at each other, shrugged as if they could not argue with this assessment even had they wanted to, and finished off the joint.

"I am not getting stoned!" Mr. Oh said. "I am trying to help my wife, and I thought you had agreed to help me."

"Preparations are necessary," Darin said. "No way can we watch that fucking thing stone cold sober."

"Don't speak of her that way!"

"Mr. Oh," Mark said gently, "he's not talking about your wife. He's talking about that thing inside her."

"How are you so calm? I expect not—"

"You *don't expect.*"

"I don't expect you to feel as I do, but you seem…" He gestured helplessly for the words. "You seem as if this is almost normal to you."

"We grew up in a small town in Utah," Darin told him. "Now we've been in Hollywood for five years. We've seen some things that seemed pretty fucking weird to us. I'd say 'almost normal' isn't too far off for this."

Mark shook his head. "I don't know, dude. I think 'almost normal' is going a little far. I think this is at least slightly weird."

"Pussy."

"Dude! Come in for pork belly hot pot, stay for Satan? Come on. That's fucking weird."

"THAT'S ENOUGH!" shouted Mr. Oh. "Yes, it is weird! But it is not a show! It is not something on TV to laugh at! If you're not going to help me, then GET OUT OF MY RESTAURANT!"

They stared at him, then looked at each other, abashed. Beneath their surprise, beneath the bland Hollywood smirks they had picked up somewhere along the way, Mr. Oh thought he could see the faces of those two young boys from Utah. Maybe that was how it was with his wife, too. Maybe she was still in there, trapped.

He remembered what he had forgotten. It was a story his grandmother had told him, a story from before the Second World War, when she was a girl living in a village a hundred miles from Seoul. It was about a kind of healer, one who healed by feeding the hungry. He knew how to do that.

"We're sorry, Mr. Oh," said Darin. "We didn't mean to make fun. We'll help however we can. Do you want us to go get a priest or something? I mean, he'd probably just tell us to fuck off, but…"

"No priest," said Mr. Oh. "We're not Catholic. We're not even religious. But we are Korean. I think I know what to do. Stay here and watch her, please."

He made several trips between the kitchen and the office, bringing in portions of each special they'd planned to serve tonight, all the *pan chan* they'd prepared, a few particularly succulent-looking raw fruits and vegetables, and last of all a new bottle of peach schnapps from the bar. He cracked the seal and set the cap on the floor beside the full bottle.

"The bottle should be made from peach wood," he said. "But I have no idea where to get such a thing in Los Angeles. This will have to do."

The two writers were huddled together at Mr. Oh's desk. They'd been happy enough to talk about movie Satans, but now that it looked as if something might actually happen, they were wide-eyed and silent.

"What are you going to do exactly?" asked Darin at last.

"I'm going to feed it."

"Feed it! Dude, that doesn't sound like the best way to—"

"It is the Korean way. My grandmother told me this. The ritual should be done by a Korean healer called a *pansu*, but I will have to do it myself."

"Still, are you sure—"

"It is not like the movie." In case the thing inside Bobbi was listening, Mr. Oh hoped he sounded more confident than he felt. "This devil does not want my wife's soul. It wants the pleasures of her body. It cannot make love or smoke or eat. It would like to do any of these things, but most of all it is hungry."

"Can we do anything?" Mark asked at last.

Mr. Oh shrugged. "I suppose it might try to jump from her to me. If it does…" He shook his head. "Take her with you, get out, and call the police."

"But—"

"Quiet, please. I'm going to start."

Bobbi's mouth opened impossibly wide, and guttural laughter spilled out. "Moron! You think you can catch me with food? Cut off your penis and feed me that; perhaps such a tiny morsel will still my hunger!"

She had spoken in Korean this time; he supposed he still had something to be thankful for. He turned away from the cot and addressed the doorway that led to the kitchen.

"God of the doorway! God of the kitchen! God of this little eating house that is our second home! Come and feast, if you will." He spoke these words first in Korean, then repeated them in English.

"I thought—" Darin began. Mark shushed him.

"Feast and make yourselves content, for I would ask a favor of you. Should this humble repast fail to satisfy, I will happily prepare as much as you require."

"It is good," said Bobbi in a new voice.

The three of them turned to look at her. Her face had changed again; the expression of rage and pain seemed to be buried somehow under one of haughty benevolence. "Your repast is good, Samuel Oh. Give it to us."

"Take it," he answered, and untied her wrists.

Bobbi rose from the cot and approached the dishes laid out on the floor. Her gait was steady, her bearing regal despite her disheveled hair and the vomit that still streaked her clothes. She knelt before the dishes and, with her fingers, delicately took up portions of each one. Mark and Darin watched with increasing wariness, as though they expected her to resume flinging food at any moment, but she simply tasted each dish and returned to the cot, where she lay down again.

"Now you have feasted," Mr. Oh said. "Now I ask a favor of you. Will you intercede with the spirit that has possessed my wife? Will you invite it to feast also, and leave us?"

"I shall try," said Bobbi in the same calm voice. "You know that such spirits will not always settle for a feast."

"I know."

She closed her eyes and lay motionless on the cot, scarcely seeming to breathe. When her eyes flew open again, they could see that the first spirit was back. It thrust out its tongue and laughed that guttural laugh. "Will you feed me, husband?"

"I am not your husband," said Mr. Oh. "I am the husband of Bobbi Oh, whose body you have stolen. But I will feed you before I ask you to leave her."

"What if I refuse to leave her?"

"There are other things that can be done," Mr. Oh told it, wondering what in the world those things might be.

"Perhaps not. Perhaps I will join you in bed tonight, Samuel Oh."

He managed to suppress a shudder, and said only, "Will you eat?"

"I will," she said. But this time her body did not rise from the cot, though she began to make chewing motions with her mouth. Mark nudged Darin and pointed at the food. Mouthfuls of it were disappearing, apparently into thin air: a clump of *kimchi*, the head of a fish, a piece of winter squash marked by invisible teeth that must have been far larger than Bobbi Oh's.

"You have eaten well," Mr. Oh said when the dishes were clean. "Will you go now?"

"I have eaten very well," the thing replied. Though Bobbi's mouth still moved, the voice now seemed to emanate from all around them. "I would like to eat so well every day. I will not go."

Mr. Oh closed his eyes for a moment. This would be the crucial moment. "You have eaten," he said, "but you have not drunk."

"Ahhh...true!"

A loud sucking sound filled the air, as if a huge rude child were finishing off an enormous ice cream soda, and the level of the peach schnapps began to sink. Mr. Oh sprang for the bottle, seized it by the neck, and screwed the cap on as tightly as it would go. The bottle jerked once, and the office fell silent.

Mr. Oh's legs failed him. He sank to the floor.

The writers stared at each other as if they had missed something. "Is that it?" said one of them; Mr. Oh wasn't sure which.

"Is what it?" said a soft, feminine, Korean-accented voice. They all turned as Bobbi sat up on the cot, frowning at her soiled outfit and the three men staring at her. She began to sob, and Mr. Oh went to her.

Mark and Darin drove down Wilshire Boulevard toward the La Brea Tar Pits. The bottle was in the trunk, taped up in a lettuce box Mr. Oh had given them, well padded with crumpled Korean-language newspapers.

"You're sure that thing isn't going to just bust out of the bottle?" Darin asked for the hundredth time.

"Dude, you heard what Mr. Oh said," Darin told him. "It's a *peach schnapps* bottle. He said peach has some kind of power over it. He said it would make the thing too weak to break the bottle."

"I hope to hell he's right."

"Hope no more, we're here." Mark pulled over and cut the engine. The tar pits had been closed for hours, but only a chain link fence separated them from the street. Mark and Darin got out, opened the trunk, unpacked the bottle, and carried it to the fence. A smell like a hundred freshly resurfaced blacktops filled the air. They cast twin apprehensive looks at each other.

"You wanna try it?" asked Mark.

"Oh, right. When we were playing Horse last week, you said I threw like a girl. This shot's all yours, buddy."

Mark got a firm grasp on the bottle's neck, stepped back from the fence, wound up a couple of times, and let fly. They held their breath as the bottle sailed over the fence. It seemed to hang suspended for several beats too long, catching the light of the street lamps and neon signs, glittering in a nasty way. Then it dropped easily into a pool of prehistoric tar and, within seconds, was sucked out of sight.

"Dude, nice shot," said Darin.

"Thanks." They returned to the car and drove away without looking back. After a few miles of empty Wilshire, Mark said, "You know, I'm still hungry."

"Yeah, me too. Let's grab something."

"Whaddaya feel like?"

"Maybe something besides Korean."

"I think so, yeah."

"How about that all-night Thai place over by Jumbo's Clown Room?"

"You got it," said Mark, and swung the car up Western toward Hollywood Boulevard.

BURN, BABY, BURN

The girl waits by the side of the road, just past Lolita-age but obviously still jailbait. She wears a pair of ragged denim cutoffs and a grubby white T-shirt bearing the logo of John Lennon's Plastic Ono Band. Her dark hair hangs stick-straight and lank to the middle of her back. July 1976, and she's pretty sure she is somewhere in New Jersey.

When a green VW bus comes along, she sticks out her thumb and watches it roll to a stop. The rear doors swing open; hands help her in. Pot smoke. Young male faces, their tufts of attempted beard and mustache like scattered weeds, barely hiding the zits. King Crimson or some other ponderous art-rock band blaring from a stereo that's probably worth way more than the van itself.

"What's your name, baby?"

"Liz."

"How old are you?"

"Seventeen," she says, adding three years. The boy looks skeptical, but Liz can tell he doesn't really care.

They offer her liquor, which she declines, and pot, which she cautiously tries because it smells so good. The end of the joint glows red as she tokes on it, so smooth, doesn't make her cough at all. She holds the twisted cigarette before her face, focusing her eyes on the small lurid point of fire.

"Hey, babe, quit bogartin' it," says another boy. "Less a'course you want to work out a trade."

The driver swivels in his seat, making the van swerve on the road. "Gas, grass, or ass, nobody rides for free." They all laugh uproariously. Liz feels a hand on her leg, then two more encircling her wrists, not squeezing yet but letting her know they are there. Letting her know she is trapped.

They wish.

Liz hasn't hurt anyone in a long time. The images that come back to her when she does it are too unbearable. She's been learning to focus her ability, to put her power into things that don't scream and hurt and die when they burn. But she is Elizabeth Anne Sherman from the Kansas side of Kansas City, and she is still a virgin, and she's damned if she is going to lose her cherry getting raped by a bunch of stoned hippies.

Among other things, she is afraid her parents might look down from Heaven and see it happening.

So she lets the heat well up from the place deep inside her, somewhere just below the center of her chest she thinks it is, and it arrows out of her in a thin, pure ray. It's spilling from her eyes, her fingertips, and it doesn't hurt her at all, it feels *good*—

The ratty boys are scrambling away from her, away from the little corona of flames around her. Liz smells scorching hair, knows it isn't her own. She gathers all her strength and reins it in, *sucks* it in. It has taken a better part of four years, but she *can* control it now, and she doesn't want to kill these stupid boys.

"Fuck!"

"She musta dropped the fuckin' doob—she's on *fire*—"

"No, man, it's comin' out her hands! Get the bitch outta here!"

The VW screeches to a halt and Liz hops out before she can be shoved. She stumbles on the shoulder of the road, steadies herself, spins and manages to shoot them the middle finger before the doors slam shut and the van takes off again. A hundred yards down the road, she sees it stop again. The back doors open and a blanket is cast out, flaming merrily.

Liz laughs.

It first happened when she was eleven. She'd always hated the ugly ginger-haired boy who lived next door. Her big brother Steve usually made the kid leave her alone, but on this sunny Saturday afternoon Steve was in his room desperately trying to finish some chemistry project that was due on Monday. Liz was playing with her Matchbox cars in the front yard when the ginger kid showed up. He wasn't smart enough to entertain himself, and when none of his equally nasty friends were around, he got off on tormenting Liz.

He leaned over her, stuck his face right in her face. He seemed all freckles and mean, squinty eyes. "Hey, *Lezzy*," he sneered. "Betcha think you look *pretty* with that stupid-looking hairstyle." Liz's mother had fixed her hair in ponytails that morning, crowning them with shiny purple holders that looked like grape-flavored candy.

The kid kicked dirt at her, overturning several of the little cars. "Fuck off," she said.

"Hey, fuck *you*, bitch! Girls ain't supposed to talk that way—so I guess you ain't much of a girl!" He grabbed one of the ponytails and yanked hard. She felt her pretty hair ornament snap, saw it tumble in the dirt. Fury swelled in her, pure and hot.

She looked up at the ginger kid, her eyes shimmering with what felt like tears, and he grinned. "Awww, look at the little *BAY*-bee—"

Then flames were coming from his mouth instead of words. He fell to his knees, clawing at his throat. Liz saw the fire take his hair, sizzle his eyes. He was burning and she was glad. He was a ball of flame, spreading to the lawn, the bushes, the house. Her rational mind was gone now; she did not know she was burning her own home and could not have stopped it if she had. She was nothing but a conduit for the beautiful, deadly fire.

The fire raced through the neighborhood, destroying her house, the ginger kid's house, more. Thirty-two people died that day, including Steve and Liz's parents. Firefighters found Liz wandering in the blackened wreckage, filthy with soot but unscathed. No one could figure out how the fire had started, though arson was suspected. No one knew how Liz had survived. She didn't know either. Though it was in her future to make fried calamari of an Elder God, Liz had no idea how great her powers were.

No one around her understood anything at all until the man from the Bureau finally came to visit.

Some nothing town called Plainville, and she's sitting in front of a cold cup of coffee in a diner when the black girl starts talking to her. "You OK, girl? You want one of these doughnuts? You don't have to pay for it—they're day-old."

Liz accepts gratefully. She hasn't eaten anything since sometime yesterday. She's also never spoken to a black person before. None had lived in the spanking-new Kansas City suburb her parents had chosen so carefully (and which she had lain waste to so easily). A few had gone to her school, but the two races kept themselves separated so completely that desegregation may as well have never happened. And there are none at the Bureau, not yet. She's a little nervous, but after some of the freaks she's met in the last few years, one black girl not much older than her isn't so scary. "Thank you," she says. The doughnut is stale, but Liz doesn't care. She makes it disappear in a matter of seconds, and the girl silently slides another onto her plate.

"Runaway, huh?"

This isn't the first time she's been out on her own, and she knows how obvious she is, a fourteen-year-old wolfing down free food like some starved stewbum. "Throwaway," she says, though it isn't strictly true.

"That's rough."

Liz doesn't know what to say. She stares at her plate, then looks back up into the girl's friendly face. It's been a while since she saw one.

"My name's Mahogany."

"I'm Liz."

They shake hands. Liz notices that Mahogany's palm is a dusty rose-pink, not brown as she would have expected. The hand is strong, the knuckles slightly swollen.

"You look so tired," Mahogany says. "If you need a place to rest for a few days, I have one."

Liz Sherman's first rule of the road: take what you have to, rides and food and such, but trust no one. "That's OK," she says. "I mean, it's really nice of you, but there's someplace I have to be."

They both know it's a lie, but Mahogany nods, says nothing more until Liz gets up to leave, and then just a soft "You take care, now."

"You too. Thanks."

Liz pushes open the greasy glass door of the diner and sees rain sheeting down. She hates the smell and the feel of rain. She wavers for a moment before realizing that she just can't make herself go back out there yet.

"You said maybe I could stay with you a few days?" she says, turning back to the counter. Mahogany smiles, and Liz feels an upsurge of something she hasn't known in years. It takes her a few moments to realize this feeling is hope.

The man from the Bureau had the kindest, saddest eyes Liz had ever seen. They sat out on the stoop of her current foster residence and he asked a lot of personal questions, including whether she had begun to menstruate yet. (She had, just three weeks before the conflagration that killed her family.) She wouldn't have answered such questions for anyone else, but she felt some undercurrent of empathy with this man, something she couldn't quite identify but couldn't ignore either.

"How's it been for you with the foster families?" he asked.

Liz shrugged. "The Svoradys were weird. They wanted

me to act like I was five years old or something. When some little kids came in, they kicked me out. Then I came here, to the Fletchers'. They were pretty nice at first, but...well, you know what happened. I guess that's why you're here."

"The accident."

Liz stared at the floor. "Yeah."

"It wasn't really an accident, was it, Liz?"

She threw herself off the stoop, trembling with anger. "*I didn't set the fire! I didn't!* I know everyone thinks I did, cause I was fighting with Donny right before it happened, but I thought maybe you were different—"

"I don't think you *set* the fire."

She stopped raging. "You don't?"

"Not with matches or a lighter. Not in a way that other people can set a fire. And I don't think you meant to do it. And hey, nobody got hurt, just a little smoke and water damage. But the fire came from you, didn't it, Liz?"

She looked up at him. He didn't seem angry or scared, just certain. "How do you know?" she whispered.

Instead of replying, the man reached into his pocket and pulled out a dollar bill. He held it in the air between them, and she saw something shimmer from his eyes.

The bill began to burn.

They watched the small flames lick at the paper for several seconds before the man let the bill fall to the ground and smothered the fire with is foot.

"I can do it too," he said simply.

A hundred questions rose up in her. "What—how do we—why—"

The man held up his hands in a placating gesture. "Plenty of time for all that and more. But first I have a proposition for you. Liz, what you have is called a 'wild talent.' Instead of being shuttled around to foster homes, would you like to live in a single place, a home, with other people who have wild talents? Would you like to learn more about yours, and how you can control it?"

She didn't have to say yes; the man could read it in her face.

"It's called the Bureau for Paranormal Research and Defense," he told her.

BURN, BABY, BURN

✦

By the time Mahogany's shift ends, the rain has slackened and the sun is beginning to dry up the puddles on the sidewalk. Mahogany says her house is only a few blocks away. They walk in a companionable silence, having spent most of the afternoon chatting while Mahogany waited on an occasional customer.

The neighborhood looks poor but well-kept, the houses painted in pastel colors, no trash in the streets and only a ghostly scrawl of sandblasted graffiti on a wall here and there. "Two more blocks," Mahogany says. "There's one thing I ought to tell you before we get there."

Liz looks up, guarded, her fragile hope beginning to crumble. This is the part where Mahogany tells her something awful, something about heroin or turning tricks maybe, and Liz will have to turn and walk away from the only person who's been kind to her in weeks. "What?"

"Well, you're not gonna be the only person staying with us. My momma and I sort of help people out, other kids who need a place to go. There's a girl there whose folks threw her out cause she's pregnant, and two boys who like each other...you know?"

Liz just says "That's cool," but she could cry with relief, except that she never cries. When they finally come to the house, a solid old two-story deal with bright red trim and a pointy roof covered in multicolored shingles, she almost feels as if she is home.

Just inside the front door, mouth-watering fragrances envelop them: basil, garlic, fresh bread. "Momma!" Mahogany calls. "I've got somebody with me!"

A woman stands at the stove stirring spaghetti sauce. As she turns, Liz sees that she looks old enough to be Mahogany's grandmother instead of her mother.

"Momma, this is my friend Liz. Liz, meet my mother, Zora."

"Welcome, sweetheart. We're pleased to have you here. You hungry?"

"I am now," Liz says.

Zora laughs, and Liz notices that her careworn face is beautiful. "Good. Mahogany, see if you can find David and Patrick. Caroline's feeling poorly; I'll take a tray up to her later. Liz, will you keep me company?"

Mahogany leaves the kitchen. Still stirring sauce, Zora gazes levelly at Liz. "We don't have too many rules around here, but there are a couple you should know. One, you don't judge anybody in this house. Only God is fit to judge, though I don't believe He does. Two, you're safe here and welcome to stay as long as you want, but if you're in some kind of trouble, I need to know about it."

"I'm not in trouble," Liz says. "Just on my own and tired." Technically it's true; though the Bureau is probably looking for her, she didn't break any laws by leaving. Her custody is a hazy, difficult matter, and the Bureau is hesitant to stir already troubled waters by hunting her down and dragging her back to Connecticut every time she gets antsy and takes off.

"Good. You don't lie to me, I won't lie to you." Zora turns back to the stove. "Can you lay out those plates for me?"

They eat at a wooden table polished to a golden-brown patina, with old-fashioned white lace placemats that remind Liz of a set her mother had. That brings a lump to her throat, but the chatter of David and Patrick, the two boys who like each other, soon distracts her. They are about fifteen, long-haired, handsome and fragile-looking. Liz wonders how they ever survived in the real world. By their wits, she supposes; both are as talkative and charming as Siamese cats. They tease Mahogany with great affection, and she gives back as good as she gets.

After washing up, the five of them sit in the living room and talk for hours. At one point Caroline comes downstairs to say hello. The bulge of her pregnancy looks impossible on her tiny frame, but she carries herself with a brittle, formal dignity. No one asks Liz any prying questions, nothing about where she came from or why.

Everything is fine until she goes to bed.

She shares Mahogany's room, which has twin beds on either side of an antique vanity table. The sheets are deliciously soft and cool, especially since she's been sleeping in bus stations and behind minimarts lately. The two girls talk a little longer about nothing in particular, just sleepy scattered conversation like the kind that comes toward the end of a slumber party. Then it's dark, and Liz is dreaming.

She's back in Kansas City, in the front yard of her house. Her Matchbox cars are scattered on the ground before her and the purple ponytail holders are in her hair. The ginger kid is nowhere in sight. She turns and goes up the front walk toward the house. The door to the foyer is partly open, but Liz can't see inside. She has almost made it to the porch when her mother half-staggers, half-falls through the door.

Her mother is in flames. Her face is barely recognizable, her eyes seared shut, her hair burned away. Her mouth stretches open and emits a soundless scream. Her charcoal-claw hands reach out to Liz.

"*Mommy*!" Liz screams. She rushes to the burning woman, trying to smother the fire with her own body, but it is too late. The flames don't burn Liz, but her embrace crumbles her mother's body and the charred pieces fall away.

She awakes to the sound of screaming, but it is not her own.

The bed is on fire. She sees Mahogany through the curtain of smoke and flames, reaching frantically for her, shouting her name. The covers are destroyed, the mattress beginning to smolder, but Liz feels nothing. She scrambles out of the bed and rushes to Mahogany, who grabs her. "Are you hurt?" Mahogany asks, and it twists Liz's heart a little that this should be her first question.

"I'm fine! Help me put this out!" Liz spins wildly, searching for clothes, covers, anything that might smother the flames.

"We can't, Liz! Look—" The fire is halfway up the wall, exposing joists and wires. Blue sparks fly as it spreads into the electrical system. The girls run from the room, down the hall, yelling and banging on doors.

Everyone gets out alive. That is her only consolation, the only reason she doesn't just throw herself in front of a fire truck. The house and everything in it are completely destroyed.

When the firemen have gone, leaving only a pile of black and stinking rubble where a home once stood, Zora and the two boys come over to Liz. Zora's arms are wrapped around the boys' thin shoulders; all three faces are streaked with soot and tears. Liz sees Mahogany comforting Caroline on the other side of the street. "The officer knows a shelter we can stay in tonight," Zora tells Liz. "I don't know what we'll do after that, but we'll find something."

Liz can hardly meet the woman's eyes. "That's OK, Zora. You guys have enough to deal with. I think I'm just gonna take off."

"In the middle of the night? Why, Liz, I can't let you—"

"I've got someone I can call to pick me up," Liz tells her.

She sits on the curb and watches them ride away in two police cars. Before they'd parted, Mahogany hugged Liz and gave her the address of some aunt or cousin, asking her to write and let them know she was all right. Liz knows she never will. These people don't need her in their lives, don't deserve what she has already given them in exchange for their kindness.

When the last police car is gone and the street is dark and silent, Liz goes to a pay phone on the corner and dials the number of the BPRD. It only rings twice before being answered by a doctor Liz knows.

"Come and get me," she says, and begins to cry. She hasn't cried since she was eleven. The tears burn worse than fire. And when the long black car that comes to fetch her finally turns into the Bureau's winding driveway, Liz knows that this time she really is home.

SYSTEM FREEZE

Plodding toward the summit of Everest, high above Camp Three where every step felt like a life's work and every breath made her pray she'd be able to take the next one, Fria Canning saw her first dead body. It was a Japanese man in a red climbing suit, huddled in a fetal position beneath an outcropping of rock. He must have been here since last season, maybe longer; at these altitudes it was almost impossible to retrieve the bodies of dead climbers, and the mountain became their sepulcher.

One of the man's mittens was gone, exposing a withered, clawlike hand. His face was dark and scoured as the rock, a grimacing mask that no longer looked human. Fria had to unclip from the ropes to get around him. As she did, she said a quick silent prayer for him, a wish that the mountain spirit Chomolungma might welcome him, and then she kept climbing.

She didn't think of the corpse again until fifteen minutes later, because fifteen minutes later she was dying.

It happened so fast, only a heartbeat to break through the deceptive crust of snow, less than that to fall a hundred feet, and then the shock of impact. Fria felt something snap in her thigh, something give in her shoulder. She'd plunged into a hidden crevasse, landed on some sort of ledge deep within the ice. Her harness had been attached to the ropes, but either her carabiners or the harness itself had failed. She couldn't move to check; hot knives of pain sliced at her when she tried.

Fria tried to assess her situation. She lay on her right side facing a wall of ice that soared up nearly as far as she could see, only a faint gray smudge of daylight wavering at the top. The outer layer of the ice was translucent, webbed here and there with white fissures. Deeper in, the ice turned a delicate, almost metallic blue. Beyond that—as deep as Fria's eye could see—was an opaque core of darkness.

If she died here, the glacier would chew her up and eventually spit her out somewhere lower on Everest. She'd heard of it before, climbers disappearing into crevasses and getting churned out months or years later. Fria didn't want that. She'd rather stay on the mountain, become part of its vast system. The idea of leaving her imprint on systems had always appealed to her, had kept her home learning to talk to computers when other kids were cruising the mall, had inspired her to write the artificial intelligence program that financed this climb.

She imagined her consciousness spiraling away from her body, into the multifaceted ice, into the matrix of the mountain. Dreamily, without fear or even surprise, she noticed that a man was coming through the ice to meet her. He walked as easily as if through thin air, wearing a well-cut black suit and dark glasses like some CIA spook. His stride was neither hurried nor hesitant.

Was this Death? She'd always imagined him as more colorful somehow. She flashed on the prayer flags that the Sherpas strung on the mountain for the wind to harry; each snap of a brightly colored flag was a prayer to an ancestor. Fria felt sure that the man approaching her could have nothing to do with such matters.

When he reached her, he bent and offered her a hand. She

grasped it without thinking, and the man pulled her up as easily as she herself might lift a toddler. She sucked in her breath, anticipating the pain of her broken parts, but the pain did not come. She realized she was standing intact on the ice ledge, supporting herself with her own sturdy legs, and the man was watching her with the barest hint of a smile.

"Hello, Fria Canning."

"Hi."

"I'm Agent John Fine, and I'm very pleased to meet you. We admire your work tremendously. AI isn't my particular specialty, but my colleagues say your Self program is the most revolutionary piece of artificial intelligence work achieved by any batt – any human."

"Well, thank you." Fria was certain now that she must be hallucinating. Probably she was dying, random bits of memory spooling through her brain like a buggy hard drive spitting out lines of nonsense code. What could she do but play along? "I'm, uh, very proud of Self. It almost feels like I created something that's more than the sum of me."

"Of course it is more than the sum of you." A trace of irritation crept into the man's voice, but he smoothed it over at once. "Fria, would you like to get out of this crevasse? Would you like to summit Everest?"

"I don't think that's in the cards."

"It can be. Do you want it?"

She laughed. "What are you, the Devil? Is this my chance to sell you my soul for another thirty or forty years on stinky old Planet Earth? I don't think so, Mister."

"What would the Devil want with an artificial intelligence program, Fria?"

"Help him recruit the damned, maybe? I don't know. Forget it. Fuck off."

The man took a step backward into the ice, and at once Fria was lying on the ledge again, limbs bent in ways they shouldn't be, the pain red and pounding and a hundred times worse than before. She began to cry from the relentlessness of it, and soon her sobs turned into retches.

"Die deep in the ice then, if you like. It makes very little difference to me either way. But I'm not the Devil, or any other such silly human bogeyman, and all I want from you is something you would have done anyway."

"What?" she managed to spit out.

"Finish the new AI program you began work on before you left for Nepal. We will contact you when it's completed, and we will pay you very handsomely for it."

"Honest?" she said, absurdly.

"Honest."

"You got it."

And then with no sense of transition she was back on the surface of the mountain, within sight of Camp Four at the base of the South Col. Her limbs were whole and strong, her gear undamaged, her climbing harness hooked onto the ropes. The man was nowhere to be seen. The whole thing might have never happened. In fact, it couldn't have. She was climbing without bottled oxygen, after all; she must have slipped into hypoxia, and her air-starved brain had taken her on one hell of a trip.

Though every cell of her body ached, she'd never felt more intensely alive.

Fria started toward Camp Four, where her Sherpa team would have hot tea and a dry tent ready. The next day just before noon, she stood upon the summit of Everest, one foot in China and the other in Nepal.

She'd been staring out the window above her desk for nearly an hour, not seeing the fields of tall grass and summer wildflowers that surrounded her house. She was picturing mountains.

With a shake of her head, Fria brought herself back to reality and forced herself to look at her computer screen. It was filled with lines of code that no longer made sense to her. She didn't know why, but she just couldn't work on this program anymore. Maybe it had too many associations with the climb, with the accident she'd had—or rather, the accident she *imagined* she'd had. Fria knew she couldn't have survived the kind of fall she remembered, let alone have gotten herself out of the crevasse and continued on to the summit.

Therefore, she'd been hypoxic—perhaps even had a touch of cerebral edema—and hallucinated the whole thing.

She was proud of having summited, but it upset her to think about Everest now. The summit was not all she'd thought it would be. The peak of her life, literally the highest point she would ever achieve, was over. Traveling back through Namche Bazaar, Kathmandu, London, New York, home, she'd felt a curious, flat depression.

She decided to put the new AI program aside. Her savings account was still healthy, and it wasn't as if she had promised the program to anybody.

The knock came two days later, catching her in her underwear, drinking cold coffee and trying to make a dent in her huge backlog of e-mail. She struggled into a ratty bathrobe and headed for the door.

She didn't recognize the man at first. With his dark suit and spook shades, he looked as incongruous on her front stoop as he had a hundred feet down in a glacier.

"Fria Canning. Agent John Fine." He offered a hand which she was too confused to shake. "I'm sure you remember me."

"Not really, Mister, uh—"

"Agent. Agent Fine. We met under rather uncomfortable circumstances—circumstances I'm sure you wouldn't want to repeat. I'm here about the AI program."

"The new one?"

Fine's silence was confirmation enough.

"I'm afraid I won't be completing that one. I've moved on to other things, and I'm not sure what business it is of yours anyway."

"We had an agreement, Miss Canning."

Then it all came back to her: the crevasse, the pain of her broken body, the searing cold. The promise she had made to the man who walked out of the ice.

"I can't do it," she whispered. "It makes me think too much of—of—"

"Of *this*?"

Fine's body was changing, glittering, a mass of proliferating crystals seeming to burst from his mouth, chest, abdomen. Ice. Ice coming out of his body, advancing like a speeded-up film of glacial encroachment. Ice touching her, surrounding her. Ice tightening around her and cracking her bones.

"We *hate* it when our batteries give out early," she heard Fine say, and then the ice covered her face and she knew no more.

✦

The coroner stepped back from the autopsy table shaking his head. "Damnedest thing. I don't understand it."

His assistant shrugged. "What? All those broken bones, looks like she was beaten to death."

"I don't know if she was beaten or not. The injuries are more consistent with a fall, but she was found in her living room—where the hell did she fall from? Anyway, the injuries didn't kill her."

"What, then?"

The coroner looked out the window for a long moment before answering.

"This woman died of hypothermia."

The window in the morgue was small, high, and dirty, but through it the coroner and his assistant could plainly see the sun and sky of a perfect July day.

BAYOU DE LA MÈRE

The bayou twisted through the green sward of Vermilion Parish, brown and slow as a snake basking in the sun. On its left bank sat the town, very small and picturesque, and just now, very very hot. The midday sun bounced off neatly whitewashed buildings and sizzled up from narrow streets like heat rising from a well-seasoned iron skillet. Ancient moss-bearded oaks made shady tunnels over the sidewalk, but if you stood in one of these tunnels too long, a small cloud of midges and mosquitoes would form around you. All in all, it seemed a hell of a place to spend an August vacation, but it had been highly recommended by the bartender.

Said bartender was spending *her* vacation in Colorado, and the two cooks intermittently cursed her name as they trudged around the little town. They had only been successful restaurateurs for about a year. Before that their existence had been pretty much hand-to-mouth, and they'd never taken a real vacation. When they decided to close the restaurant for two weeks during the slowest part of the summer, they felt as if they should go somewhere for at least a week, and friends urged them to get out of New Orleans for once in their lives.

"We can't be more than, like, four hours away," Rickey had said. "Something could come up." Mo convinced them to visit the little town, a three-hour drive from New Orleans.

They were staying on the second floor of a 160-year-old hotel that looked out over the bayou. The place smelled of lemon floor polish and genteelly decaying wood. "I gonna show you up to y'all room," said the proprietress when they checked in. The accent out here was nothing like the exuberant, full-throated New Orleans one; rather, it was low and musical, with a hint of the French spoken here less than a century ago. The woman's jet-dark eyes, curious but not overtly hostile, kept slipping back to them as she showed off the room with its double bed. *We might not like everything y'all do in New Orleans*, Rickey imagined her thinking, *but we need y'all money.*

When she had gone, G-man set his suitcase on a marble-topped end table and started unpacking. "You think she ever met a couple of fags who were less interested in all these damn antiques?" he said.

"I kinda like the bed," said Rickey. It was a wooden four-poster with knobs carved into tortured flower shapes.

"That's cause you got an interior design queen inside you, just dying to get out."

"Yeah, right." Rickey had decorated the restaurant's dining room almost singlehandedly, choosing everything from the silverware pattern to the shade of green on the walls, but he had never spent more than fifty dollars on anything for their house and couldn't imagine doing so. They weren't home often enough to enjoy nice décor.

Although it was nearing the hottest part of the day, they forced themselves out of the hotel and into the slow-baking streets. That was when they started cursing Mo's name. The bayou, the cannons in the square, the old Catholic church: all were lovely, but all seemed to waver behind a cell-thin, sticky layer of heat. G-man, whose eyes had always been painfully sensitive to light, could hardly see through his dark prescription glasses. Within thirty minutes they were in a rustic but air-conditioned oyster bar gulping cocktails even though happy hour was still far away.

"How can it be hotter here than in New Orleans?" Rickey said.

"It's not," said G-man. "We just got time to notice it here."

"We stand over goddamn stoves all day. I thought I was immune to heat."

"Y'all from New Orleans?" called the manager of the seafood restaurant, who was over in the corner playing video poker. "Y'all don't even know what real heat *is* way up there."

Rickey and G-man looked at each other in half-drunken amazement at having suddenly become Northern aggressors. "I guess that's what we get for calling Tanker a Yankee," said G-man. Their pastry chef had been born in Covington, about forty-five miles north of New Orleans.

They sat at the bar awhile longer, feeling somewhat out of place but not uncomfortably so. There was nothing obviously touristy about them; to all outward appearances they were just a couple of working-class guys in their late twenties. They both wore black chef pants—Rickey's patterned with a thin blue stripe, G-man's with a variety of mushrooms—and they might have been about to work the dinner shift, if this place were slack enough to let workers drink before shifts. However, Rickey felt sure that they were as conspicuous as a couple of dorks in Acapulco shirts with cameras hanging around their necks. He didn't really care, though. He wasn't supposed to feel like a local; he was on vacation.

The thought began to sink in as he sipped his third bourbon and soda. He was on vacation! They didn't have to worry about the restaurant for a whole week. They could drink and eat and wander around aimlessly and do whatever they liked. Thinking about it, he began to feel horny. "Let's go back to the room," he said.

Once there, they cranked up the air conditioner and pulled the curtains shut. The room filled with cool afternoon shadows. Rickey rummaged through his bag. "Did you bring the lotion?" he said.

"I thought you put it in that Ziploc bag of toothpaste and stuff."

"I don't see it." They had used hand lotion as a lubricant since they were teenagers, and had never quite graduated to K-Y, Astroglide, or any of the raunchier products.

"Well, we gotta have it or I'll be walking around here like a guy with fatal hemorrhoids," G-man said sensibly. "I saw a Wal-Mart on the way into town—we could go get some."

"Dude, I don't want to go to Wal-Mart and buy nothing but a bottle of lotion. You know how that's gonna look?"

G-man shrugged.

"Wait a sec," said Rickey, digging deeper into his suitcase. "Here it is. I forgot I put it in its own bag in case it leaked."

They undressed and lay on the bed kissing, but the alcohol, sun, and twelve straight days of work before the vacation had begun to kick in. Their caresses went from languid to exhausted. "Damn, I'm sorry," said Rickey when he realized he had just dozed for a few seconds. "I want to do it, but I can hardly keep my eyes open."

"Me neither. Maybe we could just nap for a few minutes."

They settled against each other and allowed themselves to drift off. By the time they awoke, the room was fully dark, the town outside was still, and every restaurant and bar within a twenty-mile radius had been closed for hours. They went out onto the balcony and sat smoking a joint. At the other end of the street, a traffic signal cycled through its colors several times before a lone car came along, paused briefly at the red light, then went on without waiting for the green. The bayou was invisible in the night, signaling its presence only with a damp organic smell and an occasional flash of moonlight on water.

"Let's go for a walk," said G-man.

"A what?" Rickey wasn't being a smart-ass; the concept of taking a walk late at night simply hadn't occurred to him in many years. It wasn't as dangerous as critics of New Orleans suggested, but it wasn't the sort of thing most people did if they could help it.

"I feel like stretching my legs. Then we can come back here and finish what we started."

The second-floor landing was decorated with an antique mirror, a spray of wildflowers, and a rather large, gory plaster statue of Jesus exhibiting his Sacred Heart. They walked softly down the old wooden staircase and let themselves out of the still hotel onto the silent street. "You know what's different here?" said Rickey after they had gone half a block toward the town square. "Even after a really fucking hot day, it doesn't stink. There's not that shitty garbage vapor rising off the asphalt."

"The bayou stinks a little."

"Well, what do you expect? We're still in Louisiana."

"I don't think these people even believe you and I are from Louisiana. They think New Orleans is a whole 'nother country."

"They might have something there."

"Seriously." As they neared the square, G-man looked up at the spire of the eighteenth-century church. "It's so Catholic out here. I don't think I could live in a place that takes its religion this seriously."

"What you talking about? Your mom takes religion as seriously as anybody I ever knew."

"That's what I'm talking about," said G-man. "That's why I couldn't stand to be around it. Sure, New Orleans is Catholic, but it's different there. More…I don't know…more adaptable. You're a lapsed Catholic out here, they're gonna make you think about it every damn day of your life. You never really get away from it anyway—they get you by the time you're five, they got a part of you forever."

"Yeah?" As they passed in front of the church, Rickey made a grab for G-man. "Which part?"

"Quit it!"

"How come? There's nobody out at this hour."

But G-man was looking at something on the other side of the square. Following his gaze, Rickey saw a serene-faced white statue of the Blessed Virgin Mary seated in the center of a little bubbling fountain. "Oh, no, dude. You don't want me grabbing your ass in front of *that*?"

"It's just not nice," G-man said uncomfortably.

"Sorry. I didn't know you were still ashamed of me when the goddamn Catholic Church was watching."

"Course I'm not ashamed of you. Don't even say that."

"Don't act like it then."

They walked over to the statue and examined it in silence. Rickey couldn't remember ever seeing the Virgin Mary seated before. People in New Orleans put little statues of her in half-buried bathtubs in their yards, and while her robes might be painted either the traditional blue or a more festive pink, she was always standing. He refused to ask G-man about it, though. Instead he circled the fountain and entered a small floodlit garden behind it. On the whitewashed wall of the nearby church, dozens of flesh-colored lizards lay in wait for nocturnal insects. A little door on the wall was labeled CHAPEL OF PERPETUAL ADORATION, but Rickey didn't know what that meant.

G-man followed Rickey into the garden. He saw the sign and the stained glass window beside the door, where the ornate tabernacle holding the consecrated Host cast a weirdly shaped shadow. Remembering the bland dusty taste of the Host on his tongue, he looked away. "This place makes me nervous, that's all," he said. "It's hard to explain. You remember I told you about the last time I ever went to Confession?"

"Yeah. I think that was about a week before the first time I fucked your damn brains out."

Rickey was being crude because his feelings were hurt, and G-man ignored it. "Well, that was what? Thirteen years ago? That was the last time I ever felt like the Church could see what I was doing—"

"The Church?" Rickey said dubiously. He had not been raised in any particular religion. "You mean like God, or what?"

"Sorta. Not exactly. It's more like management." The critical gaze of management was something they both understood all too well. "Like a bunch of 'em all sitting on some kind of advisory board, deciding whether your sins are venial or mortal, how many Our Fathers or Hail Marys you gotta say, counting up every filthy thing you ever done. And even if you leave the Church, your family's still Catholic, so you know you're gonna get a goddamn funeral Mass when you die."

"Dude, you're twenty-nine. What are you thinking about funeral Masses for?"

"I'm not. That's not what I'm trying to say." Frustrated, G-man turned his back on the Chapel of Perpetual Adoration. "It's just that when I walked out of that confessional, I knew it was the last time, and all of a sudden I didn't feel like they were watching any more. Out here, it kinda feels like they are again."

"Yeah, and you're not the first homo tourist they ever saw. Get over it."

They walked the rest of the way around the square in silence and turned onto the deserted Main Street, here called Rue Principale. Rickey stopped to peer through the window of a darkened restaurant. "Cheap-ass flocked wallpaper," he muttered. G-man didn't say anything, and Rickey turned on him. "Well, what? Do you hate it here cause they got a lot of serious Catholics? It's our first ever vacation. I hope you don't hate it."

"No. No, I don't hate it. I'm happy we're here. I just never been to Cajun country before. I didn't know it would be so..."

"So what?"

"Catholic."

Rickey threw up his hands in disgust and started walking back toward the hotel. G-man followed, feeling guilty. "It doesn't matter," he said after a few minutes. "It's not gonna ruin anything."

"It better not."

Neither of them said a word until they got back to the room, but it wasn't a particularly uncomfortable silence; they'd been together long enough to get annoyed with each other and get over it in the space of a few minutes. G-man was thinking about a small white rosary his mother had given him for his first Communion. He'd tried to say his penance on it after leaving the confessional for the last time, but had only been able to get through five Hail Marys before realizing he couldn't be a Catholic any more, not if what the priest had just told him was true. He'd put the rosary away and hadn't thought of it for years, until one day Rickey was looking for something in a dresser drawer and found the little velvet-lined jewelry box. Anyone would have thought Rickey had found condoms or maybe a come-stained copy of *Huge & Uncut*.

"What do you still have *that* for?" he'd demanded, and G-man finally just said in as sharp a tone as he ever used, "Look, my mom gave it to me. Shut the fuck up about it." But that wasn't the only reason he had kept the rosary. He could no more have thrown it out than Rickey could have gotten rid of his father's old Army dog tags, even though Rickey's parents had been divorced for a quarter-century and he never talked to his father.

Rickey was thinking about a conversation he'd had at the restaurant a few months ago. One of the cooks wondered aloud why G-man (who was elsewhere at the time) wouldn't try to extort a little lump crabmeat or something from a purveyor who'd sent them some wormy fish, and Rickey said, "You gotta understand, G's just a nice Catholic boy at heart." He was surprised to hear himself say that, because he always thought of G-man as his partner in crime, his lieutenant of degeneracy. Not so much in a sexual way—he supposed they were actually pretty vanilla in that respect—but they had gone through a considerable amount of liquor, drugs, scams, and sleaze during their tenure in the kitchens of New Orleans. To suddenly think of G-man in a whole different light was strange and somehow arousing. He went home that night and fucked his nice Catholic boy until they were both sore.

The hotel room felt very cold after the simmering night. The sweat on their skin turned clammy and they burrowed under the covers, shivering. "I don't know about you," said Rickey, "but I'm wide awake now."

"Same here. You want to do something?"

"Yeah."

It was years since they'd had sex in unfamiliar surroundings—usually they were lucky if they could find the time and energy to do so in their own bed. They'd done it once in the restaurant before opening night, but that was mostly just to make the place theirs, and Rickey had been too worried about the carpet to really get into it. Now, though, he found that he liked being in a strange room. There was something vaguely illicit about it, something that hinted at affairs and assignations without any of the pain these things would cause were he to actually seek them out. The mattress was a little too soft, but it was wider than the one they had at home, allowing them to roll around without fear of falling off the edge. Only after several minutes did they notice that one of the bed's wooden legs was banging quite loudly against the floor.

"Goddamn uneven floorboards," said Rickey. "Goddamn broken-down place. We should've stayed in a Holiday Inn."

"Don't worry about it," said G-man. "Here, let's try that daybed by the window."

They moved over to the daybed. "That's better," Rickey said, testing its firmness. "The springs aren't all busted in this one."

"I'm sure we'll bust 'em."

"Probably so...oh. There. You like that?"

"Yeah," said G-man. "I like that a lot." He braced himself against the windowsill as Rickey fucked him. He could barely make out the dark slow shape of the bayou through crooked oak limbs, and above it all, a crescent moon hanging high in the predawn sky. For the first time in years he remembered his mother telling him the moon was God's eye, and that whenever he saw it, he should remember God was watching him. He closed his eyes, but the white crescent's afterimage still hung there. "Let me turn over," he said to Rickey.

"Aw, c'mon G, we never do it this way—"

"OK, let me lay down then."

Rickey did. G-man pressed his face into the upholstery and concentrated on Rickey's mouth against his neck, Rickey's hand on his dick, Rickey's dick in his ass. God wasn't watching them, and if He was, it didn't matter. G-man had not stopped believing in God when he left the Church; he'd left because he did not believe that God wanted him to have a loveless life, and he'd never once felt that being with Rickey was wrong. He didn't feel it now. He just felt more self-conscious out here, somehow, than he'd ever felt in New Orleans.

They returned to the old four-poster bed to sleep, but their dreams were not peaceful. Rickey dreamed he was back at the restaurant on reopening day. Dinner service was about to start, but no one else in the kitchen had shown up, not even G-man. Rickey was on the line by himself, wondering how in hell he was going to work all the stations, trying to stifle his fury at his negligent crew because he knew it would incapacitate him if given free rein. He could already see the tickets piling up, could hear the waiters yelling for their orders. *Didn't I go on vacation?* he thought, but realized he had no memory of it.

G-man dreamed of Sts. Peter and Paul, the church he had attended as a child. His name was still Gary Stubbs, he had just barely started learning to cook, and his knees were sore from kneeling, waiting to take Communion. Again he tasted the crumbling wafer, the musky sweet wine. He could smell the sweat on the priest's palm, could count every hair on his wrist. It was supposed to be flesh, blood. Wasn't that as intimate as anything you could do with a person? He had always wondered.

It was Sts. Peter and Paul, but for some reason the Stations of the Cross were all in French. *Jésus condemné à mort...Jésus chargé de la Croix...Jésus tombe une 1e fois...* He wasn't sure if he was reading the words or if a voice was whispering them to him. The Stations themselves were set into walls that towered high above his head, the carved wooden faces of the figures precise in their anguish.

Then he was outside the church, out in the night long past even midnight Mass, and it was no longer Sts. Peter and Paul; it was the old church in the bayou town. The weirdly backlit tabernacle rose up behind the window, wavering as if an unseen figure had passed between it and the glass. The statue of the Blessed Virgin sat placidly in the center of the fountain. Her mantle and her shoulders were worn almost smooth, like the soapy-looking lambs that mark children's graves. *Jésus recontre sa Mère*, the voice whispered, or had he just thought the words? Her eyes were wide, blank, white, fixed upon him as she began to rise, her stone knees crumbling, her lap cracking apart. Her shadow appeared on the stained glass window, blotting out the tabernacle. She reached out to him—

"Jesus!" he said, sitting up in bed, his heart hammering, his right hand at his throat. A second later, he realized he was groping for the St. Christopher medal he hadn't worn since he was twelve.

"G? You OK?" He felt Rickey's hand on his back. "What's a'matter?"

"Nothing. I'm fine."
"Sure?"
"Yeah."
"C'mere…"

Rickey pulled him down and wrapped a warm arm around his chest. Fitted into the curve of Rickey's body like a spoon, G-man began to relax, his heart slowing, his eyes growing heavy again. By morning he remembered nothing of the dream, and Rickey did not remember waking at all.

Since they'd never had a proper meal the day before, they woke up ravenous and headed immediately to the oyster bar, which was just opening for lunch. "Y'all cooks?" the waitress asked, noticing the baggy shorts they had made from worn-out chef pants. In her musical half-French accent she chatted to them about local restaurants, recommended the boudin, warned them away from the crawfish stew. Throughout the meal she kept their cups filled with strong chicory coffee. By the time they finished eating, the strangeness of yesterday had receded and they felt almost comfortable in the town.

Out on the square, they stood looking up and down Rue Principale. It began to dawn on them anew that they had absolutely no responsibilities, no plans, nothing to guide them except whatever they felt like doing. "You want to check out the church?" said Rickey, though he had shown no interest in it the day before.

G-man looked up at the wooden spire. He realized he really didn't want to go in there; certainly he'd been in Catholic churches since his last Confession, but he felt a reluctance to enter this one. Almost an aversion, for what reason he couldn't imagine. "What for?" he said.

"Well, I don't know. It's old. It's one of the things you're supposed to see—Mo said so." Rickey pointed at a nearby sign. "Look, it's on the Historic Register."

"I guess," said G-man with no enthusiasm. But Rickey had already set off toward the church, apparently determined to be a dutiful tourist despite his lack of experience. G-man followed as he always had. The heavy front doors sighed shut behind them and they were enveloped in dimness, in the smell of candles and old wood. G-man could not help dipping his fingertips in the font and genuflecting as he entered; it was as automatic as brushing his teeth or wiping the edge of a plate after he had arranged food on it.

"Hey, check it out," said Rickey. "The whaddaya call 'em, the Stations of the Cross are in French."

G-man edged into a row of pews; he didn't feel quite capable of walking around the church. He sat there and watched Rickey roam around the place admiring the architecture, the history, the craftsmanship of the carved and painted wooden statues. It must be nice to enjoy such a beautiful place at face value, without the heaviness of lost faith. His head had begun to ache dully. He could not think why this church felt so much more oppressive than others he had been in.

"May I help you?" someone said. G-man looked up and saw an old priest with eyes nearly as blue as Rickey's. The priest was smiling benignly at him, offering no threat.

"Uh, we were just looking around," he said. "It's a beautiful church…Father."

"Yes, it is. You're from New Orleans?" G-man nodded. "I recognize the accent. I was pastor of St. Rosalie's in Harvey for ten years before I came here. What brings you to our town?"

"We're just tourists."

"Well, I'm so glad you stopped in. The church is very old, you know. So many stories about it. Some of them are even a little crazy." The priest chuckled. "Did you see the statue of the Blessed Virgin out front? The one by the fountain?"

"Sure. It's kinda unusual—"

"Because she's seated, right. You don't see that too often in America. The statue was carved in Italy in the style of the Pietà, but alone, without the body of Christ in her arms. It represents her sorrow after He was taken from her. Anyway, there's a legend about it."

"I bet there is," said G-man. He really didn't want to hear it, but he knew he was about to.

"It's said that the Virgin will stand if a sinner comes before her." The priest chuckled again, then broke into a hearty laugh. Up near the altar, Rickey turned to see what was going on. "But she's never stood up yet, so apparently all of us in town and all who visit us must be without sin!"

G-man rose and stumbled out of the pew. "I'm sorry, Father," he said. "The sun…" But he welcomed the sun after the shadows of the church and sat with his face turned up to it until he heard the door open behind him. He tensed, afraid it might be the priest, but it was Rickey.

"You OK?"

"Yeah."

"You sick?"

"I'm fine."

"I'm sorry I made you go in there. I guess you didn't really feel like it."

"No," said G-man. "I really didn't."

He rubbed his hands over his face. Rickey patted him on the back, and G-man could feel the worry in his touch. After a few minutes he let his head fall back against Rickey's shoulder.

Out of the corner of his eye he could see the fountain and the soft eroded shape of the statue. Its blank gaze was upon him again, but the Virgin stayed seated. He wondered if she understood that she must either sit forever or stand up for everyone in the world.

THE HEART OF NEW ORLEANS

A bar where I sometimes drink has New Orleans street scenes painted on the walls. Not cliché tourist shit like Carnival parades and jazz funerals, but regular people's views of the city: a dilapidated old shotgun house, a snowball stand, the kind of Mid-City corner grocery out of which I'd expect to see the grocer being rolled on a gurney, shot dead in a robbery that netted $26. I guess most people wouldn't imagine the dead grocer, but I see him or some equally sad variation several times a month.

I don't go to this bar too often, because I'll just be wanting to relax and drink my bourbon, and I'll catch myself making up stories about the people in the murals. That wouldn't be so bad except that the stories inevitably end in their deaths. I've always been able to look death straight in the eye, but I prefer not to do so during my off-hours. To be kicking back with a shot of Wild Turkey, to gaze at a painting of a nice old man playing dominoes and suddenly find myself imagining him in cardiac arrest—it makes me feel like I am riding on a bum trip, as people used to say and probably still do somewhere.

I have always prided myself on fulfilling my position as coroner of New Orleans with no trace of morbidity. I may never live up to my predecessor, who played a mean jazz trumpet, but I am a bit of a bon vivant in my own quiet way. I enjoy the bourbon, though seldom to excess. Fine restaurants are an important part of my life. I try to keep up with the local literary scene, once even speaking in a very general way about some of my odder cases to a group of mystery writers at the Tennessee Williams Festival. In short, I like to think that I'm not particularly death-obsessed as coroners go, nor cursed with an overactive imagination.

So I keep telling myself that the case of the Stubbs boy was just an anomaly, one of the many inexplicable but ultimately mundane things that any medical worker will encounter in the course of a long career. I tell myself that even as I slide another fragment of his heart under the microscope, and I try to stay away from the bar with the street scenes on the walls, and occasionally I have an extra drink before turning in at night.

Children's deaths are terribly hard on everyone who must deal with them, even a childless and relatively heartless bastard like me. A little body on the slab looks less natural, somehow, than the body of an adult. You know they never contemplated their mortality, never pondered when and how it would come, never went through all the maundering about life and death and the cosmos that adults think separates them from their simian brothers. Perhaps that should make the sight more bearable, but instead it only accentuates their terrible vulnerability: they never even knew it was coming, yet here they lie.

As dead children go, five-year-old Matthew Stubbs was less heartrending than many I have seen. He was not beaten to death by a parent or stepparent; he was not left to freeze in an unheated apartment while his guardians smoked crack next door; he was not shot in his mother's arms. He was simply the victim of a stupid accident far too common in south Louisiana: left alone for a few minutes while his mother checked on dinner, he let himself into a neighbor's yard, fell face-first into a wading pool, and drowned in a few inches of tepid water. That was what the officers on the scene had surmised, anyway. My job was to disprove or confirm this dreary scenario.

Matthew was a handsome little boy with dark curly hair and long eyelashes that lay damply against his livid cheeks. Aside from some whitish purge in his mouth and nostrils—a mixture of water and mucus whipped into a froth by his struggling lungs—I found no external signs of trauma on him, nothing to suggest he had been dumped in the pool rather than falling. His blood had the bright cherry-red color characteristic of oxygen deprivation. His lungs were full of more white froth, and his stomach contained only water and a few fragments of the cold spaghetti he'd reportedly had for lunch that day. This was a straightforward drowning; I saw scores of them every summer. People fell out of boats or went swimming in the Mississippi and often didn't surface until days later. For the sake of his parents, I was glad this boy hadn't been in the water long enough to show any disfigurement.

Nothing seemed strange about the case until I examined the heart. I excised it from its moorings and cupped it in my gloved hand, preparing to weigh it, when something caught my eye. I held the little organ up to the light and tilted it this way and that, trying to understand what I saw. Internal organs are as distinctive as hands or facial features, with infinite subtleties of color, shape, venation. But I'd never seen a pattern like the one that covered the entire surface of this child's heart. Hundreds and hundreds of tiny lines were somehow etched upon the muscle, spiraling from the aorta and vena cava all the way down to the tips of the ventricles. When I dissected the heart and washed out the blood that had clotted there, I saw similar marks covering its inner chambers. Bringing a piece of the tissue close to my eyes, I thought I could make out loops and spikes, as if the lines were made up of words far too small to read.

Of course that couldn't be; it was simply a strange pattern of striation in the muscle fibers. The fact that I'd never seen anything like it was of no consequence—I'd never seen a teratoma, either, until the day I found a mass of undifferentiated tissue with two baby teeth embedded in a man's left kidney. The man had lived with this inside him for fifty-seven years, dying of a wholly unrelated aneurysm. There had been no need to inform his family of the absorbed twin's existence, which was why it now floated in a jar on my desk instead of being cremated with him.

At least I had heard of teratomas, though, had read about them and seen pictures. I'd never heard of anyone whose heart looked as if someone had taken an engraving tool to it. This condition had nothing to do with Matthew Stubbs' death, though, so it concerned me only as a curiosity. I noted it into the small microphone clipped to my lapel, then preserved the organ in a container of formalin. Though it didn't relate to the cause of death, it was certainly notable enough to save. Perhaps I'd show it to my former assistant, Jeffrey, who always appreciated an anomaly. He was in medical school at Tulane now, but he had always been among the most trusted of my staff and sometimes dropped by the morgue to see how I was doing. I got the feeling he worried about me since my separation from my husband. Seymour had never formally announced that he was leaving me—he'd just gone up to New York to visit his family and kept extending the "vacation." He'd been up there for seven months now. *Typical passive-aggressive poet*, I thought when I let it enter my mind at all.

I had six other posts that day, seven the next. In the flow of gunshot wounds, car accident injuries, and heart attacks, nothing happened to remind me of one drowned little boy. I didn't think of Matthew Stubbs again until his parents showed up two days later to invite me to his funeral.

This isn't as rare as you might think. Some families would like to pretend that I and my office don't exist; never mind thinking about what we do here. But some perceive that their loved ones have shared a final, intimate relationship with me, and they want me along for one more step. I almost always find a way of gracefully declining. I would have done so in this case if Leonetta Stubbs hadn't bulldozed right over me.

For one thing, they usually call rather than dropping by. When I heard that Mr. and Mrs. Stubbs were at the morgue's front desk, I expected a lawsuit at worst, an hysterical outburst at best. I made sure there was no blood on my lab coat before going up front to see what they wanted, but I couldn't protect them from the bleak appearance or antiseptically rotten smell of the place. I never ask decedents' family members to come here if I can avoid it. To me it is part work, part home, but to many it is the material of nightmares.

Henry Stubbs was a tall honest-faced man with a dazed look in his dark eyes. Despite the Irish surname, his olive complexion and thick shock of black hair made me suspect a Sicilian mother or grandmother. Though he shook my hand and spoke politely to me, I could tell he had turned most of his grief inward, and that his wife was the driving force here. Even in mourning, Leonetta Stubbs was something of a vision. Though she couldn't have been much older than thirty-five, her black shirtwaist dress, little pillbox hat, and deep red lipstick were like things an old lady would wear. The self-conscious hipsters who have begun to take over the Bywater and Lower Ninth Ward in recent years sometimes dress similarly, but unlike them, Leonetta didn't remind me of a child playing dress-up; something about the ensemble told me she knew of no other way to present herself. I imagined a closet full of severe dresses and outdated hats, possibly even inherited from her mother.

"Dr. Brite," she said, and clasped my hand in both of her own. Until I actually looked down and saw them with my own eyes, I couldn't quite fathom that she was wearing gloves—white cotton ones that in no way went with the rest of her outfit. Outside of the newspaper's Carnival pages, I wasn't sure I had ever seen a woman wearing gloves before.

"I have been waiting on tenterhooks to speak to you," she told me.

Though the family lived in a lower-middle-class neighborhood off Elysian Fields, her voice was rich with Uptown accents. Something running along the surface of it made me know she hadn't been raised Uptown, but had worked hard to cultivate that voice.

"Thank you for taking the time to talk to us," said her husband. He had a regular gritty, yatty New Orleans accent, and those were just about the only words he said to me.

"Of course," I said. "I'm so sorry about your son. Is there something I can do for you?"

"Might we chat in your office?" Leonetta asked.

I pictured my desk covered with autopsy reports, bulletin boards full of glossy crime-scene photos, shelves crammed with models of internal organs and things in jars. "There's really no room to sit down in my office. If you'll take a chair over here, perhaps I can help you."

We settled in the hard plastic chairs common to all official waiting rooms, as if such places must provide as little comfort as possible. I gazed at Leonetta, concerned about the purpose of her visit but also frankly curious by now.

"You must think me such a dreadful mother," she said.

It wasn't what I had expected, but I'd heard it before. "Not at all. It's true that people don't realize how fast a child can get into trouble, but some accidents are unavoidable."

"Bosh," she said. "Bosh, bother, and bullshit." The expletive startled me coming out of her mouth, but no more so than the previous two words had done. Just as I'd never met anyone wearing white gloves, I had never heard anyone say "bosh" before. "Of course I should have been watching him more closely. He was my only child, you know. I only left him in the yard because I was trying to cook that wretched red gravy, and I'm not used to it. You see, I don't cook. Henry's mother thinks I should cook more. In fact, she gave me the recipe."

I couldn't help glancing at Henry, who only looked more miserable.

"I didn't know if it would boil over, or burn, or what it might do. I was only trying to prove that I could do something the rest of the family takes for granted. They're all wonderful cooks, to hear his mother tell it. Not me, though, not silly Leonetta with her airs and pretensions. I couldn't even make spaghetti sauce without letting the baby drown, could I, Henry?"

Henry Stubbs rose from the uncomfortable chair. "I'll wait in the car," he said, and disappeared through the exit door with one anguished glance back at me and his wife.

"They're not people of quality," she said with the air of

THE HEART OF NEW ORLEANS

one imparting a dirty secret. "I thought Henry would amount to something when I married him. He talked about going to law school, but that was only meant to impress me. Now he works in that damn candy factory with his father, and he'll never do anything more than that."

"Mrs. Stubbs, I hardly think—"

She went on as if I had not spoken. "My son was an exceptional child. I'm sure you could tell, even…in his condition. Doubtless there are biological differences between normal people and geniuses."

Of course I thought then of the strange patterns I had observed in the tissue of the little boy's heart, but I said nothing, wanting to neither feed nor destroy whatever delusions sustained her.

"His playschool teacher said he was gifted. His IQ couldn't even be measured with the regular tests."

"Mrs. Stubbs…"

"Oh, I know what you're going to say. Or would say if you weren't too polite. He was only five. It was too early to tell about these things. That's exactly what his father said. 'What you talking about, Leonetta? He's just a baby. He ain't no Einstein.'"

I was struck by the bitterness that came into her voice when she mentioned her husband, and also by her skill at mimicking his homely accent.

"He *was* a genius, though. Not an Einstein—his talents didn't lie in the direction of math, science, all that nonsense." With a flip of her gloved hand she dismissed entire fields of scholarly pursuit. "My son would have written great books someday. I know, because he told me so."

"He told you…?"

"Of course he could already read. He couldn't write yet, not really, but he could give dictation. He'd tell little stories and I would write them down. One day we stapled them all together in a kind of book, and he said to me, 'Momma, I'm going to write a real book someday.'

"'You are?' I asked him. 'What are you going to write about?'

"'About the true heart of New Orleans,' he told me."

My face must have expressed the skepticism I felt, for Leonetta said to me, "I know how it sounds, Doctor. Not like something a five-year-old would say. He did, though. My son was truly exceptional."

She turned wide cornflower-blue eyes upon me. While I sympathized with her loss, I had thought her a rude and arrogant woman. She'd come here looking for absolution, or at least trying to justify the carelessness that had killed her son. She had humiliated her grieving husband in front of me. Looking into her eyes, though, I saw the vulnerability she didn't mean to reveal, and I found myself identifying with it to a dangerous degree. In those eyes I thought I saw the universal futility of life, the futility we are forever trying to deny because accepting it would obviate our reasons for continuing to live. You risk your soul trying to snatch a man from death's grasp, and two years later he dies of cancer at age forty. You let a husband see parts of yourself no one else knows, and he turns his back and leaves you. You put all your love and hope into a beautiful little boy who drowns in a few inches of water. I saw terrible things in Leonetta Stubbs' eyes, but I could not look away.

"Doctor," she said, "that book will never be written. But I thank you for taking care of Matthew. Would you do one more thing for him? Would you come to his funeral?"

In that moment there was very little I could have refused her. She gave me the name of the funeral home and the time of the Mass the next day, and as I ushered her out the door, I wondered what force of nature had just rolled over me.

When I finished work late that evening, I couldn't bear the thought of my empty house. I went to the bar with the street scenes on the walls, drank two shots of bourbon, contemplated a third but knew how the media would salivate if I were pulled over for drunk driving. The crowd in the bar seemed younger than usual, and their vigor depressed me. I drove home, drank another bourbon at my kitchen table, went to bed. I thought I'd never sleep. Then, abruptly, I found myself back in the bar. An unknown but familiar-looking young man had joined me at my table. His dark hair was clipped short, his features unremarkably handsome. It was his eyes that arrested me: they were as intense as Leonetta's, but nearly black.

"It's pretty embarrassing," he said. "I mean, what a stupid way to go, in a damn wading pool. Being five years old is no excuse for stupidity."

"What happened? Why did you fall in?"

"It was just one of those things. Just one of those crazy flings. I just wanted to go wading, but somehow I tripped getting in. I remember thinking, *Oh, no big deal, I'll get up in a second, it'll be easy.* And then I tried, and…I just didn't have my body any more. Do you know what I mean? It just wasn't *there*."

"Probably you inhaled reflexively and lost consciousness. The shock can paralyze the vagus nerve—"

"No offense, Doctor, but I don't really care about the vagus nerve, or the Las Vegas nerve, or whatever you want to call it. None of it makes any difference to me."

"Is this the future? Am I seeing the life you would have lived?"

He smiled thinly. "Future? It doesn't mean anything to me. I'm five, I'm twenty-six, I'm eighty-two. I know it all." I thought I saw a look of fear cross his face, but it was gone in an instant. "There's no distinction for me, no concept of time. Nothing but an infinity of killed possibilities."

"Did you ever write that book?"

"What book?"

"Your mother said you intended to write a book. A book about the true heart of New Orleans."

"My mother says a lot of things. But the heart of New Orleans? You can see it in the face of that lady right there." He gestured toward one of the murals, at the painted figure of a white woman standing on the porch of a tiny Victorian shotgun house. Her hands were planted on her hips; a garishly patterned wrap concealed most of her ample figure. "Can you hear her? She's hollering for her kids to come in the house before it starts raining. She's saying, 'Darla! Tom—MY! Get in here before I come knock you upside da head with one a'dem bricks!' Hear her?"

His normal speaking voice wasn't as self-consciously cultured as Leonetta's, but it was a long way from downtown. When he imitated the woman calling her children, though, he seemed to *become* her for a moment, or nearly so. I could hear twenty years of cigarettes in her voice, could feel the weariness in her swollen ankles, could smell the chicory coffee, garlic, and mildew odors that permeated the little house. Apparently he hadn't just inherited his mother's talent for mimicry; he had surpassed it.

He would have surpassed it, I reminded myself, *if he had lived*. He had not lived. I had autopsied him myself, had touched his strange heart. Matthew Stubbs was laid out in a child-sized casket somewhere in the city, ready to be buried tomorrow, and this was only a dream.

Even so, it was better than the stories I had often found myself making up about the murals. He hadn't killed off the woman as I would have been compelled to do. Rather, with a few deft strokes, he had made me imagine her whole life. I began to wonder if his mother was right. Perhaps he was an exceptional child; perhaps he would grow up to write a great book about New Orleans.

Had been an exceptional child. *Would have written* a great book. Sitting here beside him, watching him sip a tall glass of beer, it was hard to remember that he would never do any of these things.

"You're right," I told him. "That is the heart of New Orleans. One of them, anyway."

"It's all written down," he said, touching the back of my hand. "Keep it safe for me, will you?"

Suddenly I was awake in a lonely bed, the cats curled near my feet more an annoyance than a comfort. A faint taste of bourbon lingered in my mouth…but of course it would; I'd had two shots at the bar and another before retiring. Pale dawn light had begun to fill the room. Knowing I would not sleep again, I rose to make coffee. Seymour had always brought me coffee in bed fixed just the way I liked it, and I could never get it quite right. Every morning as I spooned the grounds into the filter, I thought I heard Sarah Vaughan singing, "Once you told me I'd awaken with the sun—and order orange juice for one…" Too true, Sarah, but at least you could sing like God's own cello. What could I do except cut into cold flesh to offer the living cold comfort?

Not wanting to make conversation with anyone, I intended to arrive just in time for the Mass, but the visitation was still going on when I entered the funeral home on Elysian Fields Avenue. Funerals of small children tend to be sparsely attended—the children themselves haven't had time to form a large social group, and the parents' friends, who usually have kids of their own, don't like confronting the ephemerality of these young lives. But the lobby and viewing room were packed with people. From the St. Joseph prayer cards stacked on a side table, I assumed the Stubbses were Catholic, so perhaps they were an unusually large family.

I approached the casket. At least they hadn't dressed him in a suit—there are few sights more pathetically creepy than a dead child wearing a tiny suit and tie. Matthew wore children's clothes, a blue shirt and a pair of yellow overalls with Cookie Monster embroidered on the breast pocket. A white rosary twined around the fingers of one small hand. His face looked much worse than it had when I'd autopsied him, cheeks unnaturally pink from too much arterial fluid, lips sewn tightly shut, long eyelashes poking from the swollen flesh like a shrunken head's. As I turned away, I thought a sarcastic voice spoke softly in my ear: "Why do the sweetest flowers wither and fall from the stem?" But no one was there.

The Mass was dreadful, tweedling organ music and platitudes about how God's will benefits us even when we cannot understand it. I wondered how Henry and Leonetta Stubbs were supposed to have benefited from their small son's death. The mourners were required to rise and sit back down seemingly hundreds of times, and since I wasn't raised Catholic, I was always a beat behind. Several rows ahead, a handsome young man seemed to be having as much trouble as I. He looked familiar, and eventually I recognized him as a young chef who had won a James Beard award a few years ago. I am ashamed to admit that I spent the remainder of the Mass entertaining myself with memories of his fresh sardines in Galliano-laced sweet and sour sauce.

I was on my way out when Leonetta Stubbs approached me. "Dr. Brite, thank you so much for coming."

"Not at all," I said awkwardly.

"I hoped you would. I wanted to give you this—for taking care of Matthew."

She pressed a piece of folded manila paper into my hand. I unfolded it and saw a child's crayon drawing. It was crude, but I could make out the figure of a woman in front of a house and some children nearby. Below it, in an adult's handwriting, were written the words: "Darla! Tommy! Get in here before I knock you upside the head!"

"He told me what to write," said Leonetta, "and I wrote it for him. I suppose you could call it a cartoon, couldn't you?"

"Yes indeed," I said as gooseflesh rippled up my arms. "What does it mean?"

"Well, I told you that my husband doesn't make a great deal of money, and I'm afraid we live in a rather…*low-quality* neighborhood. One day the woman next door was screaming at her children to come in before it started to rain. For some reason this struck Matthew as hilarious—I suppose he liked the idea of her being so concerned for their welfare that she'd threaten them with a beating. For such a young child, he had a very well-developed sense of irony."

"I can see that." I folded the drawing and slipped it into my pocket. "Thank you, Mrs. Stubbs. Take care of yourself."

As I climbed into my car, I began to talk out loud. "Yes, absolutely, a very well-developed sense of irony. Leaving your story in a place where no one can find it until you're dead and autopsied. Or maybe you couldn't help it; maybe you were just made that way. But you must have done many drawings. What caused your mother to give me that particular one? Did you make her do it? And what am I supposed to do with your damn story anyway? What did you mean, keep it safe for you? Am I supposed to transcribe it? Publish it? Burn it? What? Why do I have to be responsible for everything?"

If Seymour were here, I could have asked him whether I might be going mad, but he was gone. I had no sense of perspective any more, nothing to measure myself against. I turned off Esplanade onto Broad Street and headed for the morgue, where a small boy's heart lay dreaming in formalin. I wondered if I would be able to read it.

A SEASON IN HECK

The summer Paul Parsons turned eighteen, he got his first serious cooking job in a restaurant called Liquor. It wasn't that he really wanted to be a cook; rather, he was in the process of deciding what he didn't want to do with his life. He thought this negative winnowing process might be easier than deciding on a single goal and sticking to it. He didn't want to go to college, at least not yet; he didn't want the proffered bottom-rung clerk job in his father's accounting firm; he didn't want to keep living with his parents if he could make enough money to move out. And he was pretty sure he didn't want to leave New Orleans. Like many natives, he felt both sustained and poisoned by it, as if the city were sapping his strength but he might wither away altogether if he tried to leave.

Paul had worked in just one restaurant before Liquor, and that was only a pizza place. But he was smart, and he was a voracious reader. Before he started applying for jobs, he spent a week reading his mother's cookbooks, checked out

Escoffier from the library, learned all about mother sauces and mirepoix and veal stock. So he was able to talk a good game. The chef knew Paul was full of shit—it became increasingly obvious during the interview—but one of their cooks had just been fired for losing a Band-Aid and not telling anybody about it until after service. They were pretty sure it hadn't ended up on a plate, but the chef, John Rickey, went to great lengths to impress upon Paul that *pretty sure* wasn't good enough.

"If he'd have told me about it *before* service, I wouldn't have fired him," Rickey said to Paul. "It would've been a huge pain in the ass—we would've had to strain the soup he made, sort through the salad greens, check his whole mise...you know what mise-en-place is, right?"

"Your setup," said Paul, silently thanking Escoffier. "Your chopped vegetables and things."

"Well, *that's* a relief anyway. I ask that on all the applications, and last week somebody thought it meant mice in the kitchen." Rickey laughed bitterly. Though he was handsome in a sharp-featured way, his intensity made him hard to look at sometimes; you got the feeling he was always gritting his teeth. "Anyway, no matter how much trouble it was, I'd have slept a whole lot better that night knowing nobody found a fucking Band-Aid in their house salad. Cause I couldn't have said, 'Oh, it was *Matt's* Band-Aid, he's the biggest shoemaker in the place,' you know? They don't care. It's *my* name on every plate that goes out—"

"That's a good idea," said G-man, Rickey's sous chef and co-owner. He had spent most of the interview sitting silently by, long skinny arms folded across his chest, watching Paul from behind a pair of dark glasses. "You should put your name on every plate. Have it painted around the rim in gold, maybe."

"Fuck you," Rickey told him without rancor. "See, Paul, G's a smartass. He's allowed to be, cause it's his name on every plate too. Everybody else, they gotta earn smartass privileges."

"I don't think I'll be needing them," Paul said. "I'm really not much of a smartass."

G-man removed the shades and blinked at Paul. "You sure you're a cook?"

No, Paul had thought at the time. *I'm not sure what the hell I am.* But the kitchen was shorthanded even though summer was the slow season, and they had decided to give him a chance, and so far he had kept his head above water. Or, rather, he had stayed out of the weeds. That was cook-talk for staying out of trouble, and he'd begun to pick up the lingo even though it made him feel like an imposter.

Paul Parsons had spent most of his life feeling like an imposter. No one ever thought he was from New Orleans, because his mother, an English teacher, had trained the accent out of him by the time he was five: no axing questions, taking out da gawbidge, or wrenching his hands in the zink for Frances Parsons's only child. No one knew he had written an entire short novel in high school—a grim and grotesque little thing set in some fantasy-Appalachian landscape, rather too heavily influenced by Flannery O'Connor—because he had never shown it to anybody. And certainly no one knew that he had never had a single convincing erotic thought about a girl.

Kitchen work only provided him with more reasons to feel like a fake. He soon became aware that the other cooks saw him as a slumming rich kid. His family wasn't rich by any means, but Rickcy and G-man had grown up in the Lower Ninth Ward, a tough blue-collar neighborhood miles away (in distance and otherwise) from the Parsons' Lakeview home. Some of the dishwashers still lived in the projects. They'd all risked life and limb in the public schools, while Paul had graduated from Brother Martin, an old-line Catholic academy.

It sometimes seemed strange to him that the relatively poor dishwashers had cars with expensive sound systems and fancy wheel rims. Paul drove a 1988 Ford Escort whose radio only picked up AM stations. Driving to work each day, he sometimes felt so lonely for a human voice that he would even listen to Rush Limbaugh. He didn't really care what Rush and his callers said. They helped him to feel less isolated in the car, in his head, in his life.

The work was hard and took his mind off other things, for which he was grateful. Because Paul was so inexperienced,

Rickey usually put him on the salad station. It was harder to fuck up there than on the hot line, but you still had to be pretty fast when the kitchen got busy. And the kitchen was almost always busy, for Liquor was one of the most popular new restaurants in the city. A write up in *Gourmet* had brought in food-loving tourists. The concept itself kept the locals coming in: every dish on the menu, from salads to dessert, contained some kind of liquor. Probably it wouldn't have gone over well in, say, California, but it was perfect for New Orleans.

Getting ready to slice Creole tomatoes one afternoon, Paul found that somebody had put a condom over his knife handle. He had never even seen an unrolled condom up close before; its lurid pink hue, powdergreasy texture, and reservoir tip appalled him. Surreptitiously he pincered it into a nearby garbage can and looked around the kitchen to see if anyone was watching him. The other cooks were busy, white-jacketed backs bent over their own tasks, paying Paul no mind. All through service he couldn't stop wondering what it meant. Could everyone else see what he barely acknowledged in himself? Was there something obviously queer about him?

The problem distracted him and made him forgetful. At one point during the second turn, Rickey came over to his station holding a plate of the marinated fresh sardine special. "You see anything *wrong* with this plate?" Rickey asked, wafting it under Paul's nose.

Paul glanced at the plate, then at Rickey. For an instant he looked straight into Rickey's eyes, which were very blue and slightly mad. Then he looked away; he'd never been good at meeting other people's gazes, and he always felt as if Rickey was pinning him with a death stare. "It looks OK to me," he admitted, his hands still moving, layering tomato slices on a row of plates.

"You don't see anything *missing*?"

"Oh. Uh, the toasted capers?"

"Bingo," said Rickey. He set the plate down in the middle of Paul's station and walked away, tossing a final imprecation over his shoulder: "That's the third special I had to send back to you. I see a fourth one, I'm gonna break down and cry."

Paul scattered capers over the anchovy plate, finished his

row of tomato salads, and paused to take a few deep breaths. Shake, the older cook working the cold-appetizer station beside him, glanced over in concern. "You OK, kid? You need me to take over?"

"No," said Paul, abashed. "Jeez, am I that bad? You think I need to leave my station just because I forgot the toasted capers?"

"Nah, you were just looking a little toasted there yourself. Don't worry about it. Here, want an almond?"

Paul didn't, but in order to be friendly, he took the small white object Shake offered him. He bit into it and his eyes watered: it was not a blanched almond, but a raw, peeled clove of garlic. Shake howled at the look on his face, and Paul tried to laugh. He told himself that this second prank probably meant Shake had also put the condom on his knife, but he didn't really believe it. It seemed far more probable that everybody was out to get him.

※

The trouble with having a restaurant whose menu revolved around liquor, Rickey thought, was the pressure to keep topping yourself. He believed most of his repeat customers came back because the food was always very good, often great, and not infrequently perfect; he'd never been interested in leaning on the gimmick. But this was arguably the most alcoholic city in the world, and he couldn't deny that the gimmick attracted new diners. He had found that running an ad in the newspaper's Friday entertainment section guaranteed an extra-busy weekend, especially if the ad mentioned a new dish ("Cognac Poule Grand-mère") or a featured spirit ("Irish Whiskey Tasting Menu").

So tonight he sat in the bar after service resting his tired feet, sipping Wild Turkey, and picking the brains of his crew for strange libations. G-man sprawled in the booth beside him, making notes on a clipboard.

"Advocaat," suggested Mo, the bartender.

"We had some of that in our test kitchen before we opened," said Rickey. "Couldn't do anything with it. It was gross. Reminded me of some two-dollar-a-bottle eggnog I drank in Poughkeepsie one time."

"What were you doing in Poughkeepsie?"

"I don't want to talk about it."

"Well, what about Strega?"

"Too flowery."

Mo rolled her eyes and kept rinsing glasses in the bar sink.

"Maybe something with lamb and crème de menthe?" said Shake.

"Why reinterpret a cliché?"

"Why ask us for ideas at all?" said Shake, exasperated. "You know you're just gonna do exactly what you want, same as ever. You might listen to G-man, but you're not gonna listen to us."

"I listen to you. I can't help it if your idea sucks."

"How about absinthe?" said the new kid, Paul. It was the first thing he'd said since coming into the bar. Rickey looked over at him, balanced uncomfortably on a stool. Uncomfortable: that was the word for Paul. He was a clear-eyed, good-looking, polite kid, but something about him worked Rickey's nerves. It wasn't a matter of hostility; Rickey knew Paul was having a hard time and tried to be gentler with him than he was with the other cooks. But Rickey was not a calm person by nature, and having a nervous cook around made him nervous too.

"Absinthe?" said G-man. "I thought that stuff had been illegal since 1890 or so."

"1912, actually," said Paul. "But you can order it from Spain. I read that Customs doesn't care as long as you're just getting a few bottles."

"But doesn't it taste about the same as Herbsaint or Pernod?" said Rickey.

"Well, yeah, I think so. But it's a lot more glamorous."

"Huh," said Rickey dubiously. "Glamorous to who? Isn't it kind of, like, a French Quarter club thing? I don't want a bunch of those spooky goth kids coming in here looking to get drunk on absinthe. They'll scare off the other customers."

Paul shrugged.

"I don't think we need to worry about turning into a goth

hangout," said G-man. "I think it's a pretty good idea. It's eye-catching. We advertise absinthe dishes, it'll make people curious."

"Well, maybe," said Rickey. He never liked to commit himself to a new idea too quickly, especially if it was somebody else's idea. He finished his Wild Turkey, got another, and tried to stop thinking about work. The conversation moved on to other things. Paul didn't join in. After a while Rickey noticed him talking to Mo, but soon after that he got up and left.

"That kid's never gonna make it as a cook," said Shake when Paul had gone.

"He's not so bad," said Rickey. "He didn't know much when we hired him, but he's picking it up real fast."

"That's not what I mean. He can do kitchen work, but he doesn't *belong* in a kitchen. Know what I mean? He's out of place. He can't even kid around. I tried to prank him a little today, just to loosen him up, and he never even said anything about it."

"What are you talking about?" said Rickey. "What'd you do to him?"

Shake explained about putting the condom on Paul's knife handle and offering him the almond/garlic clove. Rickey tried not to laugh, but he couldn't help it. "What are you gonna do to him tomorrow? Put Tabasco in his drink?"

"Hey, that's a good one."

"I was kidding, Shake. If he can't take it, you better leave him alone."

"Yeah, yeah, I know. It's no fun picking on him anyway if he's just gonna stand there looking *wounded*."

"He'll loosen up," Rickey started to say, but a huge yawn interrupted him.

G-man laid his hand on the back of Rickey's neck. "I guess I better get this one home," he said.

⁕

Paul didn't know what made him mention absinthe. He'd never tasted the stuff, but as he spoke up, names like

Baudelaire, Rimbaud, and Verlaine danced sensuously in his head. Afterward, he felt gratified because Rickey hadn't shot down his idea as quickly as the others. Maybe he was getting somewhere as a cook. He tried to think of absinthe dishes he could suggest if Rickey asked him, but nothing came to mind except a version of oysters Rockefeller, which Rickey was certainly capable of coming up with on his own.

He sipped his beer and studied the doings of the crew in the bar. Mo was polishing glasses and sliding them into an overhead rack. Shake was talking to Terrance the grill guy, one of the biggest, blackest men Paul had ever seen. Rickey and G-man were still sitting together in a booth drinking bourbon. Paul's eye passed over them as it had done a hundred times before, but something—their posture, their proximity, who knew?—made him stop, look again, then watch them more closely. Rickey said something to G-man, and they both laughed; then G-man put his arm around Rickey's shoulders. Rickey laid his head back against G-man's arm, closed his eyes, and sighed. It was a small, simple gesture, but it was also intensely familiar: not the casual camaraderie of cooks but the easy intimacy of old lovers.

Paul sat there on his barstool, stunned. He knew vaguely that they had worked together for a long time, and now that he thought about it, he even knew that they lived together. But the restaurant was relatively new; he had assumed they just shared a house to save money. He gulped at his beer. Then, unable to help himself, he leaned over and said softly to Mo, "Are Rickey and G-man a couple?"

She gave him a strange look. "Well, sure they are. I thought everybody knew that."

"I didn't."

"It's not a big deal, but it's no secret. I hope you don't have some kind of *problem* with it." She paused, looking more carefully at him. "No, I don't guess you do. Haven't you ever met any gay people before?"

"No," he said truthfully. "I mean, well, not that I knew of."

"But you grew up here, right? Don't you ever go to the Quarter or anything? I mean…you didn't think you were the only one?"

A SEASON IN HECK

Panic tightened Paul's throat. "I don't know what you're talking about. Sorry if I asked too many questions."

"Paul, I didn't mean—"

"It's OK," said Paul, levering himself up from the barstool. His face was hot, his knees alarmingly weak. "I just need to get home, is all. It's been a long night."

He managed to get out to the parking lot and sat for several minutes in his car with the window wound down, letting the night air bathe his face. He felt simultaneously thrilled and terrified, as if he were on the verge of discovering some great landscape but the risks involved in getting there were enormous.

Paul had heard horror stories about the staff meals at other restaurants: canned beans and boiled hot dogs, two-day-old pasta, even the skimmed-off raft of ground beef and egg white used to clarify consommé. Liquor always had good staff meals, but sometimes Rickey seemed to get into a rut. He was in one now; it had been fried chicken for three of the past five days, spaghetti for the other two. Before his shift, Paul stopped off at a neighborhood place near the racetrack. "Whatcha need, dawlin'?" the waitress asked him. He ordered a roast beef po-boy and sat at the bar listening to old track habitués talk about odds and backstretches and trifectas, things Paul felt privately certain he could never understand even if he dropped everything else and took a year-long course in them. Then he pretended to watch the boxing match on the bar TV, but when everyone else groaned or said "Good one!" he had no idea what had happened.

He went on to work even though his shift didn't start for an hour. Rickey was having a heated phone conversation with somebody—probably a purveyor—and just waved at him. Paul buttoned up his white jacket, stowed his knife bag at his station, and went looking for something to do. He found G-man wiping down shelves in the walk-in cooler. "Hi," he said, feeling shyer and more awkward than ever.

G-man turned and peered at him over the tops of dark

shades. At first Paul had thought these shades were an affectation, but it turned out that G-man just had defective, light-sensitive eyes. "Hey there," he said. "You're awful early, aren't you?"

"I didn't have anything better to do." Paul pointed at the bucket of disinfectant. "I can do that for you if you want."

"Aw, that's OK. I don't mind cleaning—it gets my head clear for the dinner rush."

"Well, I could help you."

"If you're hot to wipe down shelves, I'm not gonna stop you." G-man wrung out a sponge and tossed it to Paul. Paul bobbled it, nearly got it, then dropped it on the floor. He didn't look at G-man as he began wiping shelves.

"Hey, I heard Shake was dogging you yesterday. He's just trying to make you feel at home, in his own retarded way. You shouldn't let him bother you."

"It's OK," said Paul. He hesitated, then decided to take the plunge. "I, uh, at first I wondered if he was picking on me because he thought I was gay."

"He *better* not be." G-man straightened up, knuckling the small of his back. "Did he say anything like that?"

"No…not at all."

"Good. We can't have that kinda stuff going on around here. Rickey would freak. When he was in cooking school, he once punched a guy out for calling him a faggot."

"I didn't know he went to cooking school."

"Well, that was pretty much the end of his school days. After that we just worked in a bunch of different restaurants, learned the ropes that way. We've had a few people say stupid shit, but nobody ever really picked on us for being, you know, together."

"It must've made things easier on you, having each other."

"It sure as hell did. I mean, I don't even know if I'd still *be* a cook if it wasn't for Rickey. I'd probably just be an old drunk laying in the gutter somewhere."

Paul tried to imagine the easygoing G-man as a drunk lying in a gutter, but he could not do it.

"You don't believe me now, but you should've seen me when Rickey was away at school. I was a mess."

"You guys have been together a long time, huh?"

"Yeah, we got lucky early on." G-man wiped the last shelf and dropped his sponge in the bucket. "But it just takes a little longer for most people. It'll happen for you."

"I don't even know how it happens."

"Listen, we didn't know shit either. You'll figure it out."

"I guess."

"You told your family yet?"

"I've never told anybody except you just now."

G-man reached up, took off his shades, and blinked at Paul several times before putting them back on. "I'm the first person you ever came out to?"

"Well, yeah."

"Damn. I'm flattered and all, but why me?"

"I don't know anybody else."

"What about Rickey?"

"I'm kind of scared of Rickey," Paul admitted. "He's so…you know…*dramatic*. I mean, you plate the special wrong, and next thing you know it's like a Russian novel around here."

G-man rubbed his chin thoughtfully, but Paul got the feeling he was trying not to laugh. "Presentation is very important to Rickey," he said at last. "He's not really a hardass, though. Well, he is when he needs to be, but he's got a good heart. You can talk to him about stuff."

"I'd rather talk to you. Just talk," Paul said quickly, for he thought he saw a flicker of alarm behind the shades. "I'm not some kind of psycho. I know you're with Rickey."

"So you're not gonna boil my bunny, huh?"

"Hey, you're the sous chef. I won't boil anything unless you tell me to."

G-man laughed, the tension was broken, and Paul could hardly believe he'd gotten through this conversation. He wished G-man was actually his friend instead of just his boss, but that seemed unattainable; he could not escape the conviction that people like G-man, Rickey, Mo, and even Shake existed on a different plane, blithely aware of things he would never understand no matter how long he lived or what experiences he had. Still, by gathering all his courage he was able to say, "Maybe I could talk to you again sometime?"

"Sure. You can talk to me any time you want. So are they sending us new tomatoes or what?" This last was addressed not to Paul, but to Rickey, who had just entered the walk-in.

"Dude, I don't even know. I'm so sick of those fuckers. I called Favre Brothers and asked them to send us over a couple cases, so if City Produce brings us any, I'm just gonna send 'em right back…" Rickey noticed Paul standing there. He looked at G-man, looked back at Paul, frowned a little. "What's going on?"

"Paul was just talking to me about some stuff," said G-man. "I think we got it all squared away now."

"Anything I need to know about?"

"Not really."

"Good. I don't need any more problems today. I gotta get started on those galantines. Paul, you know how to make a galantine?"

"Uh, no I don't."

"You even know what a galantine is?"

Paul racked his brain, but Escoffier seemed to have deserted him. "No," he said.

"That's good. You don't know something, you admit it. I can work with that. Well, c'mon—you get to do something new today."

It certainly seems to be that kind of day, Paul thought as he followed Rickey back into the kitchen.

It was not in Rickey's nature to leave things alone when he could worry about them, but occasionally something got past him. He didn't mention the scene in the walk-in until they were driving home late that night, by which time G-man had almost forgotten about it.

"So what was going on with you and Paul today?" Rickey said.

"What do you mean?" said G-man. He wasn't being coy; he honestly didn't know what Rickey was talking about. G-man had been on saute tonight, the busiest station in the kitchen. Now, half-dozing in the passenger seat, he had begun to dream of putting endless redfish filets into endless sizzling skillets.

"When y'all were in the walk-in. I just caught the tail end of it, but it sounded kinda, I don't know, *intimate*."

"Well, uh." Struggling to wake up, G-man wound down the car window and let air blow over his face. Even at four in the morning the temperature hovered around eighty, and the air wasn't very refreshing. "Paul likes boys," he said. "In theory, anyway. I didn't get the idea he'd ever actually slept with one."

"So what? He's looking to remedy that?"

"I don't know! He didn't tell me what he was looking for. I think he mostly just wanted to talk to somebody who's in a good relationship, you know? Like us? I think that made him feel better."

"Huh," said Rickey.

"Huh nothing. C'mon, Rickey. You really think you got anything to worry about?"

G-man looked over at Rickey, who was scowling through the windshield at the deserted cityscape of Louisiana Avenue. He'd been helplessly in love with Rickey since he was sixteen and still thought Rickey was the best-looking guy he'd ever met, so these little insecurities always caught him by surprise.

"I saw the way he was looking at you," Rickey said. "He's got a crush."

"What if he does? He's just a kid."

"He's a *cute* kid."

"I don't care if he's goddamn Harry Connick Junior. I don't even look at other people that way. You know that."

"I guess. But I still don't like it when they look at you."

G-man shrugged. "Can I help it if I'm irresistible?"

And modest too, he expected Rickey to say, or something like it. They could almost always joke about anything. But Rickey just lifted the corner of his mouth in what was obviously meant to pass as a smile but—had he showed a fraction of an inch more tooth—might have been called a snarl. G-man figured they were both tired and decided to let it go.

"I ordered that absinthe today," said Rickey, making peace.

"Yeah? Who carries it?"

"Nobody around here. I got it off the Internet from Spain. Thought we'd have a tasting for the kitchen crew when it gets here."

Now they were pulling up in front of their little shotgun house on Marengo Street. "Cool," said G-man as they heaved their weary bodies out of the car. "What dishes you thinking about doing?"

"I got no idea—that's why I want to have a tasting. See, I never really liked Herbsaint or any of that stuff. I remember going out to dinner with my folks when I was real little, and my dad would give me a sip of his Sazerac to teach me not to be an alcoholic."

"I don't think it worked."

"Yeah, but I never drink Sazeracs or pastis or any of that crap—they taste like poison to me. Like the black jellybean if you took the sugar out and replaced it with bug spray. I think Paul's probably right that it'll appeal to people, though, so I want to see what we can come up with."

Once inside, Rickey flopped down on the couch and thumbed the TV remote. G-man headed for the bathroom, peeled off his check pants and the sweaty T-shirt he'd worn under his chef jacket all night, dropped everything in the laundry hamper, and stepped into the shower. The warm spray stung his skin and slowly loosened his muscles. A miasma of food smells billowed through the steam for a few minutes, then began to dissipate.

He was still standing there, clean now but uneager to move, when he heard Rickey enter the bathroom. He figured Rickey was just going to brush his teeth or take a piss, but Rickey undressed quickly and climbed into the shower with him. "I'm almost done," said G-man. Instead of answering, Rickey grabbed his wrists and pushed him against the shower wall.

G-man rolled his eyes. It was always the same: when they argued, when things seemed less secure than usual between them, and especially when there was any jealousy involved, Rickey had this need to pin him down and fuck him really roughly. He would apologize afterward, and seem to feel remorse, but he would do it again next time. It was one of the few things G-man didn't love about their relationship, but it didn't happen that often, and since the sex was great otherwise, he had made himself get used to this. "Can we at least get out of the shower?" he said.

"No, c'mon, it's nice in here," said Rickey, biting him on the shoulder and sticking a wet finger up his ass. G-man moaned, more out of sheer weariness at the idea of having to stand up while Rickey fucked him than from any kind of passion.

"Tell me you love me," Rickey said.

"Course I love you." With his face so close to the wall, G-man could see tiny blooms of mildew in the lines of grout between the tiles. He closed his eyes. He'd never really liked being fucked from behind; it felt impersonal. You couldn't kiss, and instead of your lover's face, all you saw was pillowcases, car seatcovers, spots of mildew on shower walls.

"Just me?"

"No, Rickey, you and the entire goddamn Saints defensive line."

Rickey made him pay for that remark by gripping his hipbones hard enough to leave bruises and entering him with only a little soap for lubrication. G-man braced himself more securely against the wall, thinking how cute it would be if they slipped and cracked their skulls open. He was thoroughly exasperated with Rickey, wished he had never gotten in the shower, and felt quite irritated to realize that he was about to come anyway.

Don't you ever go to the Quarter? Mo had asked, as if it were just that easy. Well, maybe it was. Paul stood on a balcony whose ornate wrought iron curlicues had been decorated with hundreds of pairs of pink Mardi Gras beads. The bar was called Rawbones, and it had taken him thirty minutes to gather enough courage to enter the place. The cigarette smoke and earsplitting dance music had soon driven him out here. He sipped his Coke and wondered what Rickey and G-man were doing right now. How nice it would be to go home with someone every night, wake up with him every morning, and not need to go looking for love in places like this. The thought made him feel lonelier than ever.

Though the balcony was crowded, no one spoke to Paul. Maybe he gave off some sort of people-repelling vibe here just as he seemed to do at work. Maybe he was doomed to a lifetime of envying other people's relationships and renting videos with titles like "Rump Riders." He noticed two men furiously making out at the other end of the balcony and watched them until a trio of tall-haired drag queens moved into his line of sight, blocking the view. Still depressed and now horny, Paul left the balcony, navigated the narrow staircase, and exited the bar.

He'd never minded the smell of the French Quarter when he came here with his parents or with friends. There was always grease and old beer and an undertone of wet creeping fungus, but tonight it all seemed overlaid with the aroma of fresh shit, rich and cloying. The pools of light around the gas lamps had a jaundiced glow. This was a bad night, Paul decided; they happened in New Orleans sometimes, without rhyme or reason, nights where everything felt askew and the wisest thing you could do was stay home. He started walking back to his car, but he'd only gone a few steps when a voice said, "You looking for something, baby?"

Something about the guy seemed wrong immediately, but Paul figured he was just letting his perception of the night color his first impression. "I don't know," he said, trying to look at the guy without prejudice. He was a young white man, older than Paul but surely no more than twenty-five, not quite clean-looking but certainly not ugly.

The guy scanned Paul's face nervously, then glanced at his crotch. "You want a blowjob?"

"I don't think so."

"Hey, don't get the wrong idea. I ain't no hustler. I just happen to like your face. Might like the rest of you too."

"Well, I mean...I'm not into doing it on the street."

"I know where we can get a nice clean room for twenty dollars."

A SEASON IN HECK

"Yeah, right." Paul might not be too streetwise, but he knew there was no decent room to be had anywhere near the French Quarter for twenty dollars.

"It's a friend of mine's house. He just makes a little extra money helping out guys like us, who want to hook up but can't afford no fancy hotel room. C'mon...I can tell you want to."

The guy reached out and took Paul's hand, stepped in close, and kissed him softly on the mouth. He tasted of spearmint and stale beer. Paul's stomach rolled over, whether from revulsion or desire he wasn't sure. Even though he figured there was at least a fifty percent chance that the guy would somehow cheat him out of the twenty dollars without delivering the promised blowjob, he was on the verge of going along with it: he was that horny. But all at once he remembered his image of Rickey and G-man at home. Probably they were asleep by now. That was the kind of thing he wanted, a lover who would fall asleep and wake up with him, not a blowjob in some stranger's rented room. He realized with dismay that he had already wasted his first kiss.

"Look, that's OK," he said, stepping away from the guy. "I think I'll just go on home."

"No, c'mon, baby—you promised."

"I did not *promise*," said Paul. The whine in the guy's voice was annoying, but at least now he had no doubt that this was just another French Quarter scam.

"Can you spare the twenty anyway?"

Paul laughed. He couldn't help it.

"Well, how about five?"

Paul might have given him five dollars, but he knew he only had a pair of twenties in his wallet. "Sorry," he said, turning away. He worried that the guy would try to follow him, but there were no footsteps in his wake. He had nearly reached the corner when the guy called after him, "Fuck you, faggot! I hope you get AIDS!"

Beautiful, Paul thought. *I'll have to tell Mo how well her suggestion worked out.* But he knew he would tell no one about this night. In any event, the next time he saw Mo, he was in no shape to tell her anything.

"Mandatory drinking session?" said Shake, reading from the bulletin board where Rickey posted things he wanted the kitchen crew to see. "How can a drinking session be mandatory?"

"I once worked at a place that had Alcohol Poisoning Night," said Terrance, who was standing beside him. "They'd put up a flyer in the kitchen every week: 'Remember, Friday is Alcohol Poisoning Night. Show up to drink after hours or experience the punishment.'"

"What was the punishment?"

"Having a bunch of hungover motherfuckers laying on your leg during service the next day."

"That's why I scheduled the absinthe tasting for tonight," said Rickey, coming up behind them. "Everybody can have a day to recover." Liquor was closed tomorrow.

"Absinthe tasting—that sounds so elegant," said Shake. "I've had absinthe, and I can tell you there's nothing elegant about what's gonna happen tonight."

"Where you had it?" said Terrance.

"In Croatia."

"What the hell were you doing in Croatia?"

"I got family there. My last name's Vojtaskovic, you know? My grandparents been working Plaquemines Parish oyster beds since 1922."

"I never knew that," said Rickey. "Are their beds any good?"

"They sold 'em all when they retired. My parents didn't care about oysters—they went into the pest control business. You know those ads that go, 'Don't let termites cave your wall in—Dial five two two six thousand, dawlin'?' That's my folks."

"No shit?" said Terrance and Rickey in unison.

"No shit."

They were all silent for a moment, perhaps wondering if the Vojtaskovic termite jingle was fated to run through their heads for the rest of the day. Then Rickey said, "I never heard of Croatian absinthe."

"I think it was from Prague. I don't remember too much

about the evening, though. We had a couple glasses with the special slotted spoon and the little sugar cube and all, and I remember thinking how civilized it was, and next thing you know I wake up six hours later in the emergency room, laying on a cot that's soaked in my own blood."

"Damn."

"So you might want to be careful about this 'mandatory' shit," said Shake. "I mean, look at Paul. I don't know if he can handle it, and he's underage anyway."

"Dude," said Rickey, "the absinthe was Paul's idea. I gotta let him try it, at least."

"Well, just keep an eye on him."

"Sounds to me like somebody better keep an eye on *you*," Terrance told Shake.

Rickey walked away, not particularly worried about any of it. One thing he'd learned about running a restaurant was that shit would either hit the fan or it wouldn't, and if you worried about it all the time, you'd quickly drive yourself insane. You prevented what you could, did triage when you had to, and commended the rest to the whims of the universe. Everybody thought he was such a control freak, and to a certain degree everybody was right. But only G-man had any idea how much he forced himself to rein it in and simply let things be.

Service ended at eleven, and after they'd finished breaking down the kitchen, everybody met in the bar. Mo cracked the seal on the first bottle of absinthe and handed it to Rickey, who had a row of highball glasses, a pitcher of water, a bowl of sugar, a pile of tasting spoons, and a cigarette lighter arranged on a nearby table. He poured a hefty shot of absinthe into one of the glasses. It was a dull, pallid green, not the garish poison-color he'd expected. Its sickly-sweet aroma drifted up to him, the smell of Sazeracs, the smell of being four years old and sitting in a restaurant booster seat listening to his parents argue. It made him remember what it was like to be utterly at the mercy of a grown-up world he couldn't understand.

I do not have a good feeling about this shit, Rickey realized, but he shook it off. Absinthe dishes would be glamorous, would bring in business. That was the important thing, not some hazy childhood trauma.

He scooped up a spoonful of sugar and dipped it lightly in the absinthe, so that the sugar absorbed some of the liquor rather than dissolving into it. Then he held the lighter's flame beneath the spoon until the sugar began to bubble and caramelize.

"What's this junkie shit?" said Shake. "That's not how we did it in Dubrovnik."

"You're not in Dubrovnik," Rickey pointed out. "I don't have little slotted spoons and I don't have sugar cubes. It said on the Internet you could do it like this."

He dunked the spoon into the glass and poured a slow stream of cold water over it. An opalescent cloud bloomed within the depths of the liquor and spread, turning it a thick yellow-green. Now it looked just as vile as Rickey had expected it to. He beckoned to Paul. "First one's yours."

Everybody watched Paul take the first sip, as if he might drop dead at Rickey's feet. "It's good," he said, and polished off a quarter of the glass.

Rickey kept trying to get into the idea of drinking absinthe, but he had only the vaguest idea of its history: names like Rimbaud, Verlaine, and Manet meant little to a boy with a New Orleans public school education, and the Old Absinthe House Bar was just another Bourbon Street tourist trap to him. He knew the glamour was there, but he couldn't see it, and *damn*, did he ever hate the taste. He'd always liked cooking with Herbsaint—just a touch of it added a nice, fragrant edge to certain dishes—but he couldn't see why anybody wanted to drink it. This stuff was twice as strong, and sweet the way some medicines were sweet, the sugar only there to half-conceal some unfathomable bitterness. Still, he had called everyone here to drink it, so he knew he had to keep drinking too.

At least Paul seemed to like it. Rickey could see him at the other end of the bar talking animatedly to Mo and her boyfriend Tanker, the pastry chef. Maybe coming up with this idea would bring the kid out of his shell a little.

Looking around the bar, Rickey realized he was the soberest person here. He was not used to such a circumstance—in fact, he couldn't remember the last time it had happened—and he found it unsettling.

G-man sat down beside him holding a fresh glass of absinthe—his third, Rickey thought. "Dude, this shit is *good*," he said, and Rickey felt more forlorn than ever. He lifted his own glass and sipped at it with renewed determination, wishing like hell for a shot of Wild Turkey.

✦

Paul knew how to drink. He wasn't in the same league as these guys, most of whom seemed to have been abusing alcohol since they were twelve or so, but drinking was just something you learned to do when you grew up in New Orleans. He had heard that at Tulane you could tell out-of-state freshmen from the local ones by their drinking habits: the expats binged and got sick, while the local kids had mostly learned to pace themselves.

So he wasn't too surprised at how well he took to the absinthe. Midway through his second glass, he found himself talking to Tanker and Mo in a way he would never have been able to do while drunk on some other, more ordinary libation. "Where you went to school?" he asked them. The broad yatty inflection that had begun to creep into his voice amused and abashed him, but he couldn't seem to rein it in. If his mother could hear him right now, she'd have him reciting elocution exercises for weeks. This struck him as funny, and he tried to explain it to Mo and Tanker. "She used to make me say, 'The bird laid an egg while standing on her leg,'" he told them.

They laughed. "Da boid laid a aig while standin awn huh laig," Tanker repeated, exaggerating the accent he already had.

It was strange how the absinthe buzz worked. In one part of his mind, Paul was stone-cold sober, casting a dignified eye upon his own behavior, congratulating himself for making the others laugh, calculating what he might say next that would be even funnier. In another part, he felt as isolated as ever, but that no longer seemed like a bad thing—rather, it was like being in a well-lit cozy room on a cold night, catching safe glimpses of the outside world through little mullioned windowpanes.

He had another drink and began to imagine himself in a Parisian café circa 1899. Shake, across the room, looked a little like Oscar Wilde—not in his glory days but as a broken old man, after his release from Reading Gaol, disgraced and waiting to die. The thought of Shake as Oscar Wilde made him laugh out loud. Tanker and Mo wanted to know what was funny and Paul attempted to tell them, but this time they only looked puzzled. "I think I read *The Picture of Dorian Gray* in English class," said Mo.

"I never even heard of Oscar Wilde, but I heard of Oscar Mayer," Tanker said obscurely.

Well, it was all right—William Faulkner had cultivated friendships with uneducated working people, hadn't he? Paul told himself these encounters would do him good later in life. He wandered over to where Rickey and G-man were sitting in their usual booth. Rickey was staring rather morosely into a half-full glass of absinthe. "There's five more bottles of this nasty-ass shit behind the bar," he said when Paul came up. "I sure hope you can think of some good recipes for it."

"I already thought of one," said Paul. "Put sugar in it. Then put water in it. Then drink it." He laughed. G-man started laughing too, and Rickey glowered at them.

"Let's make absinthe gumbo," said G-man. "It'll give new meaning to *gumbo z'herbes*."

"How about absinthe jambalaya?"

"Absinthe roast beef po-boy. You could soak the bread—"

"Crawfish boiled in absinthe!"

"You fuckers are just hilarious," said Rickey, "but I got paperwork to do. Let me outta here." He shoved at G-man, who was sitting on the outside of the booth, but G-man blocked his way.

"C'mon, dude. Don't go. You're just in a bad mood cause you're sober. Why don't you have some bourbon?"

G-man looked up at Paul. "Would you mind getting him a double shot of Wild Turkey on the rocks?"

"Sure," said Paul, and wove his way off toward the bar. As

he went, he heard Rickey say, "I just can't *drink* this shit. It's making me feel like a pussy and poisoning me both at the same time."

Bringing back the glass of Wild Turkey (which had come out somewhat larger than a double, but he figured Rickey wouldn't complain), Paul saw himself as the chosen cupbearer who would save Rickey from the clutches of sobriety. He set the glass in front of Rickey, who picked it up and tossed back half of it. "Ahhh. That's better."

"Sorry my idea didn't work out so well," Paul said.

"Aw, no, it's working out great. Look around—everybody else likes it. I'm just a picky bastard. G and Tanker will come up with some ideas even if nobody else does."

"Hey," said G-man with the air of one about to impart some vital piece of wisdom. "Hey, listen, you guys. What if …" He laughed.

"What if what?" said Rickey.

"What if we all get so hung over that none of us can ever stand to think about absinthe again, let alone cook with it?"

"Then I guess it'll be up to me," said Rickey, polishing off his bourbon. "Why not? Everything else is."

G-man rolled his eyes at Paul. Paul laughed, which got G-man started again. "Jesus fuck," said Rickey. "I see I'm gonna have to hit the Turkey pretty hard to catch up with you two."

"Lemme get you another one," said Paul.

"That's OK, I got it. Y'all constitute a hazard walking around here."

Rickey slid out of the booth. G-man let him go this time, then grinned across the table at Paul. "I love that guy," he said.

"I know. You're so lucky."

"I know I am." G-man looked a little teary-eyed for a moment. He recovered and downed the rest of his drink. Paul wondered whether to tell G-man about his encounter in the French Quarter, but he didn't feel like talking about it. Instead he said, "Is it really romantic being with the same person for so long?"

"Romantic?" G-man appeared to think about it. "No, it's

not romantic exactly. It's, like, coffee cups and laundry and who's driving today. You know what I mean?"

"Not at all."

"It's…" G-man waved his hands around as if trying to snatch the right word out of the air. "It's *comfortable*," he said.

"I see."

"No, shit, that sounds so boring. It's not boring at all. You know what?" G-man leaned across the table. "You have sex with the same person for fourteen years, it doesn't get boring at all. It gets *better*."

"Really?" Paul wanted to hear more.

"Yeah," said G-man, sounding a little awed. "I never would've thought it could. I mean, it was pretty great to start with. But jeez, Rickey…" G-man glanced around, but Rickey was over at the bar talking to Shake and Terrance. "He just does me right, man."

"That's great," said Paul, hoping for more details but unsure how to ask.

"And goddamn, it's not like I got much basis for comparison, but he must be the dick-sucking champion of the world. The guy has no gag reflex."

"That sounds pretty comfortable, all right."

Paul, however, did not feel comfortable. He was suddenly, painfully horny. His hard-on had escaped somehow from the fly of his underwear and was scraping unpleasantly against the rough-stitched inner crotch seam of his checks. He couldn't even excuse himself to do anything about it, for he was sure it would be visible to the entire bar. Beneath the edge of the table and G-man's line of sight, he put his hand down to adjust himself. The warm pressure of his palm offered a little relief, so he left it there. "So is it true what they say about tops and bottoms?" he asked.

"I don't know. What do they say?"

"Well…I mean…is that really how most relationships work?"

"I don't think it's *absolute*. You're with somebody long enough, you're gonna try just about everything. But yeah, mostly you end up doing one thing or the other." G-man grinned. "Guess that makes me a bottom, huh?"

"Does it, uh, does it, does it hurt?"

"Oh, jeez no. It's fucking awesome. Except..." Behind the dark glasses, a shadow seemed to cross G-man's eyes. "I never have really liked getting it from behind. It just feels impersonal."

"What about...what about being a top? What's that like?"

"Well." G-man shifted in the booth, and for the first time it occurred to Paul that he might be getting turned on too. "I never fucked Rickey until after he came back from cooking school. We got an apartment together, and the first night we slept there, he was like, 'You wanna do something we never done before?' So we did. I thought..." G-man sighed. "I kinda thought he'd met somebody up there, in New York, and maybe they fucked him and he liked it. Some older guy who really knew what he was doing. He said a couple things that made me wonder...But if he'd done that, I didn't think he would've come home and slept with me. We never used any protection. Eventually we talked about it, and it turned out there *was* an older guy, a celebrity chef. Cooper Stark—remember him?"

"Never heard of him," Paul said.

G-man looked pleased. "No reason you should—trendy early-nineties New York shit, that's all. Sun-dried cherries and kiwifruit. Anyway, Rickey didn't sleep with him. Told the guy he couldn't—he wanted to be faithful to me. And I couldn't really say anything, because I'd almost ended up fucking a go-go boy in the Quarter while he was gone—that's what kinda shape *I* was in. So we worked it out. We worked a lot of things out. That's just what you do if you want to stay together."

"I guess you don't have much choice," said Paul.

"God, listen to me. How'd I get going about that? This is some drink." G-man peered into his empty glass. "I need another one."

"Well, here you go," said Rickey, coming back to the table and setting down fresh drinks for all three of them. "How'd you get going about what?"

"Huh?"

"You just said to Paul, 'How'd I get going about that?' Then you said you needed another drink." Rickey slid back into the booth. "That was all I heard."

"Oh," said G-man, looking lost. "Well…"

"He was just telling me how long you've been together," said Paul.

"That's true," said G-man, relieved.

"Jeez, why're you talking about that for? Paul doesn't want to hear—"

"Dude, shut the fuck up." G-man leaned over and kissed Rickey on the mouth. Rickey tried to pull away, but G-man grabbed the back of his head and held him there, and after a second Rickey gave in. Paul saw their tongues touch. He imagined himself right in the middle of that, pressed down harder with the palm of his hand, and felt his dick throb one, two, three times as he came. He'd rearranged himself enough that most of it went down his pants leg, and as he felt it trickling into his sock and staining the top of his leather workboot, he felt like the sleaziest person in the world.

✢

"Oh my God," said G-man. "Please, please kill me. If you love me, please just shoot me in the head."

It was the next afternoon, and they were just waking up. Even if Rickey had wanted to shoot G-man in the head, it would have been difficult to do so, as G-man's head was mostly hidden under a heap of pillows and blankets.

"Little hungover?" Rickey asked.

"This isn't a hangover. This is…" G-man considered. "Purgatory, at least."

"What? I can't hear you." Rickey yanked the pillows away. G-man groaned and clapped his hands over his eyes. "Turn off that light!"

"Dude, that's the sun."

G-man found enough strength to crawl across the bed and lay his head on Rickey's lap. "I don't think I like absinthe after all," he said.

"I told you that shit was nasty."

"I did think of a good dish, but I can't remember it. I wrote it down, though. There should be a napkin in my pants pocket."

Rickey got up, found G-man's pants, and extracted a bar napkin from one pocket. "'AB TH PAP FIN,'" he read aloud. "'TAKE 1 AB BOIL W/IT. STIR TARR SALT MORE STOCK. TOP BUTT. X2 = 45.' That's great, G. I'll get right on that."

"Fuck you."

"I'm glad you made sure to note that X2 = 45. Since I suck at math, I never would've known that."

"Blow me."

"I'd be happy to," said Rickey, unperturbed. "But are you sure you feel up to it?"

"Oh my God…that reminds me of something. I had this weird conversation with Paul. You heard the tail end of it, remember?"

"Sorta. What was so weird about it?"

"Well, I think he might have been jacking off."

"Say *what*?"

"I didn't know if I ought to tell you, but I thought you might've seen it too, and I didn't want you to get the wrong idea or anything. We were just talking, but it seemed like he got kinda excited."

"Well, what were you talking about?"

"I can't remember," G-man said honestly. "I think I might've said something about how long you and I been together."

"Damn, you *were* drunk," Rickey said. "I can imagine a lot of weird shit going on in that bar, but in my wildest dreams I can't imagine that nice boy Paul Parsons sitting there jacking off while you talked to him about, like, the longevity of our relationship."

"Stranger things have happened," said G-man, a little wounded by Rickey's skepticism.

Rickey narrowed his eyes. "What's with you, anyway? You *like* the idea of him getting off on that?"

"No! God…I was just trying to be honest."

"Seems like you kinda like it."

"Rickey, I don't like anything right now, OK? I like the

fact that we don't have to go to work today. I'd like to sleep about six more hours. Quit being a dick and let me go back to sleep."

"The whole thing's just gross," Rickey said to the pillow that G-man had pulled back over his head. "I mean, the idea of somebody *fantasizing* about us. It's fucking perverted, is what it is. It's a matter of *privacy*." He plucked at the pillowcase. "You think I should fire him?"

Unlike his bosses, Paul remembered everything. Even at the height of his drunkenness, a hideous clarity had remained. He was assailed by images of himself in the bar, hanging like some groupie on G-man's every word, shamelessly manipulating his crabbed organ, soaking his own sock and shoe with ill-gotten ejaculate. But had G-man seen him do it? Even worse, had Rickey? Paul didn't know, and it tormented him.

Even now, though, he couldn't shake his fantasies of how differently the evening might have gone. If only G-man had said to him, "Come home with us, Paul—we'll teach you everything." Just the idea of them taking turns deep-kissing him was such a powerful stimulus that he could hardly get past it to speculate on the carnal delights that might have followed. He wondered if he had some sort of authority fetish, but then wouldn't he be fixated on policemen and soldiers and such? Rickey and G-man weren't very authoritarian.

Whatever it was, Paul decided, he would have to put in his notice. Even if they hadn't noticed him disgracing himself, he didn't think he could bear to keep working for them. It wasn't as though he had ever been much use in the kitchen anyway.

Though he was not a practicing Catholic, the concept of penance was deeply ingrained in him. He hauled himself out of bed, drove to Audubon Park, and set off running the three-mile loop between St. Charles Avenue and the river. The first mile or so was pure agony, but by the time he got past the zoo, some of the poison had been purged from his body and he merely felt loathsome. He forced himself up the levee, along the riverfront, and past the fields where children were playing softball and soccer, imagining how the parents would shriek with horror and snatch up their precious infants if they knew what kind of bloated pervert was jogging by. His hair tumbled greasily into his face. He could smell himself, a noxious mixture of sweat and grain alcohol. He had never felt less attractive in his life.

He hit the downside of the levee and saw a train trundling along the tracks that separated Audubon Park proper from its little riverfront adjunct, Avenger Park. Several cars, bikers, and other runners were paused near the crossing barrier, waiting for the train to pass. Paul stood there too, dripping and panting, head bowed against the powerful midday sun. He thought he might vomit and wondered if he could make it back up the levee to the little grove of trees there.

"Hey, you look about done in," said a voice behind him. "Want some water?"

Paul turned and saw a vision straddling a battered old Schwinn ten-speed. The young man had a bandanna tied around his head like Rickey did in the kitchen, but while Rickey's bandanna was as blue as his eyes, this guy's red one offset his dark hair and fair complexion. Though he'd been riding in the summer heat, he was not at all flushed; he looked as cool and collected as a prince sitting in an air-conditioned castle. He smiled at Paul and held out a bottle of spring water. Paul looked at the frosty drops of condensation on its side, then reached out and took it. His fingers touched the young man's, which were deliciously cold.

"You can finish it if you want to," the young man said when Paul had drunk half the water and tried to hand the bottle back. "You look like you could use it."

"Thanks," said Paul. He polished off the water and stood there awkwardly, wondering whether to speak again. The guy was good-looking and friendly, true, but he was probably just being kind. That'd surely change if Paul said the wrong thing. Probably he wasn't even gay.

"I'm Keith," said the guy.

"Paul."

Keith stuck out his hand. Paul grasped it and they shook.

Once their hands had met, they didn't seem overly eager to let go. Their palms slid slowly apart; their fingertips remained in contact a few seconds longer than was strictly necessary.

"You go to Tulane?" said Keith.

"Uh, no...no, I took a year off after high school. I might apply next semester, though." As he spoke, Paul realized it was what he should do. He belonged in college. Who else would want him?

"That's cool. I'm in my second year here—pre-med. I transferred from University of Texas."

"You don't sound like you're from Texas."

"You don't sound like you from Nuh Wallins, dawl," said Keith in a perfect Yat accent. Paul stared at him for a second, then burst out laughing.

"My mom's a teacher," he explained. "I wasn't allowed to talk like that."

"Oh, God!" Keith rolled his eyes theatrically. "Count yourself lucky. *My* mom's a psychiatrist, and I've never been allowed to exhibit a single neurosis without having it analyzed to death. It's a good thing she doesn't consider being gay a neurosis."

They gazed at each other for a long moment. Finally Paul couldn't take the prolonged eye contact any longer. Looking away, he saw that the train had passed and all the other people who'd been waiting were gone.

"I, uh, I guess we can get across now," he said.

"Yeah. Hey, if you're not seeing anybody, could I get your number?"

"I don't have anything to write on."

"I'll remember it."

As Paul recited the digits of his phone number, he wondered how Keith had known he was gay. It occurred to him that maybe Keith hadn't known but had just taken a chance, and he wondered where a person got that kind of courage. Was it something that came naturally, or something you had to learn? Maybe he was on the verge of finding out.

"Call me," he surprised himself by saying as Keith began to pedal away.

"Don't worry," Keith called over his shoulder. "I will."

Paul watched the slender form disappear into the live oaks' mossy shadow. His head pounded, his stomach roiled, and his body still felt like the aftermath of a fire in a distillery, but in spite of all that, he felt pretty good. With the empty water bottle clutched in his hand, he began to run again.